I'll See You in the Morning

Morning

A Novel

I'll See You in the Morning

A Novel

By

Riwen Forester

ISBN: 1-4107-0902-7 (e-book)
ISBN: 1-4107-0903-5 (Paperback)

Library of Congress Control Number: 2002096907

This book is printed on acid free paper.

Printed in the United States of America
Bloomington, IN

1stBooks – rev. 10/10/03

**Dedicated to all those
who experienced beautiful,
yet traumatic and unresolved
first love.**

Contents

Page

On the Russian Steppes 1

Love Made in Heaven 41

Interlude 123

I'll See You in the Morning...131

Part I

On the Russian Steppes

Riwen Forester

1

The sounds of the piano flooded the house. Even the occasional unplanned rests or the still too frequent mistakes, which exposed as yet untrained fingers, could not hide the fact that this piano was being played with unusual vigor and aggression. At times it seemed that the strings of the imported grand piano might break under the attack of the insistent hammering delivered by the restless hands at work on the keyboard. Rachmaninoff's piano *Prelude* in G Minor, it appeared, had never been played with such force. But then, Marta had never experienced such feelings as she had in the last few days. It was obvious that she was seeking relief from an unknown something. And it did feel good to fill the library, the hall, and the upstairs with the sounds of the *Prelude*. The only other activities that provided her with relief from tension and anxiety were ice skating and a ride with her beloved team of horses.

This library was a special place for Marta. It was the room most other people would call the great room in their homes. Her father had converted it into this special sanctuary. The tall ceilings made way for countless books and pictures. The rolling ladder used to access books stored up high had always been a fun plaything ever since she could remember, and the scar on her left cheek was evidence of careless climbing without permission, long ago. But today that ladder was a set of stairs to new and unexplored horizons. The dark, polished oak paneling gave the entire room an aura of sacredness. Here among these books there were so many words, yet none spoke unless opened and read, and then they spoke at the pleasure of the reader, of any subject, at any time, at any pace. The tall, narrow windows on two walls gave light, yet the closing of the shades only enhanced the sacred feel of the room. Pictures were hung here and there against the dark woodwork so as to point out the contrasting light of the paintings. She particularly liked the picture of the Czar family, which had been in that place as long as she could remember.

Even though the Czar had been deposed two years before, she was sure the picture would remain, perhaps as a silent sign of disbelief of the great changes taking place in the Russian Motherland. It seemed like everybody else also had a picture of the Czar and his family in their homes, but this one was special. It was special because her father had told her that when he was younger, the Czar had come to the region to visit the settlement. He had been a guest of the family and had been hosted in this very room. Everybody knew that this was special, but then everything about Marta's family, what they did and had, was special.

Although she had been playing for the last thirty minutes, she suddenly recalled that she must pay attention to *how* she was playing. She had only a few days to practice and become somewhat more proficient before her piano teacher, Olga, would come again. Surely Father would remind her of this anyway at dinner time, but she had practiced those techniques Olga had insisted on so many times. In any case, she did feel good about the other piece, Chopin's *Nocturne* for piano in G Major. Her mother, who had taught her the first fingerings on the piano, would have been proud of her if she could only hear her play these pieces.

Selma Ekk had died of childbed fever in 1914 when Marta was only nine. Doctors from far and wide, each with a different expertise, had come, but to no avail. Both her mother and the infant had died that dreadful day.

The double funeral had been a huge community event with many people in and out of the house. The ministers spoke long and loud at the large church, and again at the gravesite. She thought the choirs, which also sang at both places, sang with such dragging, extending the notes on forever. It didn't even sound good.

Aunts and uncles came from everywhere, many trying to relate to her, but she felt numb and sorry for her father when she watched his grim face. Her parents had buried two infants before, one a few years ago, and one before Marta was even born. But that seemed routine to have children die in infancy. Marta and her older, married brother were the only children left. Father would now plunge even deeper into his business affairs, but never marry again.

Soon after the funeral all relatives and friends departed, leaving Marta motherless at the age of nine. Somehow, she did seem to get used to it. In the six years since then others had, in part, replaced the functions her mother used to perform.

Marta did like Olga, because, like with her mother, the two talked a lot about music. They also made music together with four-hand pieces, and once had gone to a concert in Zaparoyhze, and once in Odessa. Olga personified for Marta the grand and glorious, the beautiful and abstract, the world beyond. She had helped her develop a feeling for music both to interpret properly and to let it speak and sing to her. An initial mechanical fingering of the piano had gradually been transformed to an art where the piano became a means of expressing feelings translated from the printed page of notes to the sounds of music.

A sense of relief did finally come over her. It was nice to be able to retreat to the safety of the familiar piano during the confusion of new feelings welling up in her. Music gave her a firm anchor, a solid post to hang onto. She could not identify what it was; it was new, it was strange, but this new feeling was also nice. The only thing she was sure of was that the stirrings from within her had something to do with Mr. Tilitzki, who had just left again that morning.

Mr. Tilitzki, or Aaron as he had insisted she call him, had been coming for occasional visits with her father for as long as she could remember. They were business associates, but she did not know what they were discussing when he came every three or four months. It was easy for her to recall when he had come ten years ago, when she was only five, and had always asked for her. The minute he walked into the house she came running to him and with a single swing he lifted her up and threw her into the air, catching her as she came flying down. Her wide eyes spoke of fear superseded with delight, for she knew she could count on him. Aaron always did nice things for her. He always brought her something. At first it was candy, chocolates, and before Christmas a special gift. On her dresser she still displayed the china doll set he had given her six years ago when her mother had died. In recent times, he still brought sweet things, but more likely now it was books, music, a picture, or a special souvenir from Odessa.

She had fun when he came and she was sad when he and Father had to go to the study to do business. But she was comforted by the fact that he always took a walk with her before he left the next day to return to Odessa. That anticipation had not changed, even today, when, at fifteen, she had grown to stand as tall as his shoulders.

5

He had just left first thing this morning and their walk the afternoon before, she thought, had been different. They had walked to the garden as usual, but coming to a newly dug trench, Aaron stepped over and reached his hand back over the trench for hers. As he pulled her over into the flower garden, for just an extra moment, he continued to hold her hand. The warm hold seemed to her to be strong and full of pulsating life. He continued the touch and Marta, at first having expected a quick release, somehow now did not expect it, neither did she want it, and secretly hoped that the touch would last.

Something warm moved within her—new, strange, and beautiful. They walked quietly past trees and shrubs deep into the garden. In this large garden the sights, sounds, and smells gave way to color, aroma, and quietness. A new Marta was born that evening. What had been a little girl now became a young woman, who experienced something new within her. She liked the feeling of that dark, handsome man, almost fifteen years her senior, walking next to her. She had, of course, always liked him for his self-assuredness, his confident walk, his proper dress, and his happy dealings with Father. Aaron and her father were obviously friends even though there was a considerable age difference. They both seemed to need and enjoy each other.

She thought he might say something, visit with her, as he usually did, but he remained quiet and she decided to follow suit. Though their hands had released, they walked close to each other.

"I guess we better return to the house."

She was glad he had finally said something, but did not respond except to say, "Okay."

Their walk took them through the rest of the garden, around the barn, and back to the house, as usual. Yet, it was quite unusual. She felt different, she felt grown up, she felt special and honored, and she did not want him to leave.

The hammered chords of the *Prelude* did somehow give relief to a new and strange emptiness inside her. Aaron was gone.

2

Life for her in the village of Rosenthal on the Crimean steppes of Russia was privileged and different and because of that, often hard. The house she lived in was much bigger than those of her friends. No one had a two-story house like she did. While the general room layout was fairly standard, the functions of many rooms were different. The great room had become the library, the summer room was a study/office, and the corner room was a guest bedroom. Family living quarters were upstairs where she had her own room, unheard of for other families with many more children in the house. Life was also different because of the private piano lessons, the periodic trips to Moscow, and the special schooling for Marta in the Girl's School. The Ekk family was obviously well to do. It was nice. She really did not know another way of life, but it did seem to limit the friends she had or the activities she could engage in.

Father was likely the most influential man in the community, and, although he was considered understanding and generous, he was known for his firm business dealings and his insistence on top performance, efficiency, and accuracy. He was driven by a passion for precision whether it was in the tidiness of the house, the running of the farm, the breeding of horses, or the dealings in his import business.

The farm in Rosenthal was really a double farm. Some years ago the adjoining property came up for sale and Johann Ekk had decided to invest in it. Although a village regulation blocked double ownership, he was able, through his power of persuasion and cleverness of the arrangement he proposed, to make the deal possible anyway. So, another family was living in the house, but the running of the affairs of the farm was under the control of Mr. Ekk. It was a large estate with additional land behind the village-controlled boundaries. Some three thousand sheep, fifty yoke of oxen, and forty horses were tended along with cattle and smaller farm animals. Some goats and a donkey were usually mixed in with the sheep as the large herd was led down toward the river for grazing.

The buildings on the estate began with the majestic home facing the street. Attached to it, and moving toward the back, was the barn followed by the machine shed. Across the yard were the garage, a cattle barn, and the haystack. Behind this continuous row were the vegetable and orchard gardens. The provision of feed and food for this large operation was a year-round effort overseen by Ivan, the foreman, and his team of farm helpers. Johann Ekk had designed a carefully planned system of canals fed by the small stream leading into the farm. This canal supported the standard well, and for backup, an artesian well. The lake behind the farm was also fed by a canal and had become an integral part of life on the estate. In the summer, it provided water for livestock; in the winter, it provided ice for the icehouse for later use, and a wonderful surface for skating. It was here that Marta had fallen countless times, but finally become one of the best skaters.

From the lake, it was possible to skate to the stream using the frozen canal—and who knows, if one would follow the stream it eventually might lead to the Dniepr River, which fed into the Black Sea.

Johann Ekk had done very well using the inheritance from his father and combining it with his keen sense of business intuition. Years ago he had begun to import horses from Oldenburg, Germany, and had successfully bred a line much sought after in his community. Through careful readings and preparation, and use of medication to prevent diseases, the herd grew in numbers and quality. He also imported machinery, stoves, and most recently a Daimler, the only car in Rosenthal. His fruit orchard had plums, apples, walnuts, and blueberries, which were of the best imported stock, and had been grafted and tended under his strict supervision. This showpiece was set among a U-shaped plantation of protective oaks, which became a favorite haven for crows that continuously announced their happiness with loud croaking and howling.

Just two years ago Johann had learned to manufacture vinegar, which quickly became widely known and desired; in quality, it was second to none and was therefore essentially without competition. It seemed that everything he tackled flourished under his management. Johann was very successful.

Natasha came in to make sure Marta got ready for school. In years gone by Natasha had dressed her every day and substituted for her mother where she could. It was Natasha who had taught Marta how to make her hair shine with much combing and how to braid it in different styles. Marta still liked braids, it gave the hair control, but also it gave her a chance to show off her artistry. She liked school quite well, even though most of her girlfriends no longer attended school, having stopped at the expected age of fourteen to help and learn in the household in preparation for hoped-for marriage. While most of the school subjects were about house-holding, which she did enjoy, she also took a special liking to history, geometry, and art. Her grades were good.

"You better get going, Marta." Natasha spoke Low German, the language of their forefathers. She had a hard time getting used to the idea that nowadays she could trust Marta to watch the time.

"Ivan has the team ready."

Kukla and Mishka, the horses of her favorite team, seemed like close friends. They knew her commands, knew the road, knew each other, and in their trot produced such a comforting rhythm. Always willing to serve her, they seemed infinitely patient to wait in the schoolyard for the end of classes, and then were even more eager to return her home.

Marta swung easily into the carriage and let the team run freely. She left behind the squealing of the pigs fighting for first rights at the trough, the happy chatter of the ducks, the clanging and pounding of the blacksmith, and the draft horses' eager calling for rest and water. She just knew this would be a good day.

The one-handed clock on the wall in the foyer pointed to somewhere shortly after three. Its long, brass pendulum swung back and forth, forever urging the connected mechanism to keep its intricate assembly of wheels and levers in perpetual motion. At the top of the hour, it would undergo its most complex series of movements: gonging out the hour count while continuing to keep the time. It had sounded three gongs when Olga arrived on the estate and now at about three fifteen, Marta returned from school. It was a happy reunion after a month's absence. Olga provided a curious mix of mature female companionship, mothering, and guiding discipline.

Olga always brought into the home a new idea, a possibility, or the announcement of an upcoming event somewhere in the world of culture.

"How are you?" Olga seemed genuinely interested.

"I am fine, and you?" Marta had learned to ask about others.

"I am fine and I brought you some great music. Are you ready to do some playing, Marta?"

"Let's have a snack first."

It really was a better idea in the minds of both. It would provide their minds and bodies rest and quietness from just completed busy activities, and prepare the mood for good music. Sometimes Marta wondered if perhaps her father and Olga might someday... But no, theirs was a platonic relationship supported by mutual respect, love for music, and a common concern for Marta.

They ate and talked while happily enjoying each other's company.

"How about if you play a bit of the *Nocturne*, just for review?"

Again, the sounds of piano music filled the house as though announcing to the world that the estate was at peace. Such had always been the message, whether after times of high happiness, dark sadness, or just to celebrate a happy routine, the strings of the piano made public the private feeling that all was well.

"I think we now ought to work on the *Prelude*."

Marta knew this was the primary assignment and soon found herself deep into Rachmaninoff. Skipping around the work from section to section, the easier ones first, she could feel that this was a composer whom she had felt before. It was nice to anticipate how the moods should be expressed.

"Let me play this section for you."

She liked to watch and listen to Olga. It was as though the music empowered Olga's hands to float freely. Truly it was hard to tell whether the music made the hands flow so lightly, or whether indeed the hands made the music sound so smooth. It would be a long time, Marta was sure, before she could play so well and make it appear so free of effort.

The lesson was finished, at least until later that evening, when they would have another lesson, since Olga came from so far and would not come for another month.

"Tell me, Marta, how are things going?" Olga always gave opportunity to talk about things beyond the piano. She knew that over the years she had won Marta's confidence, yet it was hard to nourish and maintain it with such infrequent and short contacts. It took a while to go beyond superficial topics, but when deep down feelings begged for disclosure, the reminder that there would be a lack of continuity often stifled the needed sharing.

"I am fine."

"You seem so radiant. Your eyes shine with a special glow. You must be happy?"

"Yes." Really, she wished she knew how to express the ecstasy of a few days ago, but in the end chose not to.

It had been a long time since she had really confided in Olga. In fact, it had been about four years, when she entered puberty and had noticed some profound changes taking place in her body that they had really talked. Olga had been wise in helping her learn what was happening, and helpful in preparing Natasha to assist Marta. What Marta discovered at first had been frightening, but Natasha was understanding and seemed unconcerned. That made Marta feel she carried the potential for something special. Whatever it was, she did not want to miss it.

She spent much time in the library reading. The encyclopedia seemed to talk about these things only in scientific terms, but then she discovered the Old Testament, which gave much insight into basic human drives. Lying on her bed she read in Leviticus 15 about unclean bodily discharges. She read about forbidden sexual practices, about the purification of women after childbirth, and about powerful sexual attractions described between Joseph and Potiphar's wife, between David and Bathsheba, David and Abigail, and David and Michal. She liked the small details in the Old Testament descriptions. Her body stirred as she found the passage relating the rape of Dinah, and in 2. Samuel 13 the rape of Tamar by Amnon. All of this somehow explained the purposes of what was going on in her body, and it began to expose for her the awesome excitement that might one day come. She remembered that while talking with her girlfriends she had heard stories about it—about boys and their doings. It sounded strange, frightening yet adventuresome. She now knew that there was an exciting, though apparently secret, part of life yet to come. She did not want to miss it. She wanted it.

3

Johann Ekk became increasingly concerned about the political climate in his beloved country. He had come through much turmoil in his life. World War I had begun in 1914 and ravaged the land and its people. Though Rosenthal was far removed from the violence, it was affected. Men had been butchered in unspeakable cruelty. And it seemed that mothers released their sons, wives gave up their husbands, and girls sacrificed their loves to the ongoing violence. Life seemed utterly cheap and the god of war had an insatiable appetite for blood and more lives. As the war concluded, the prayed-for peace did not appear to come to the Motherland. A new political climate fermented throughout the land, and when one wind of social change blew past, another political thundercloud was given birth on the horizon.

This is not the way it was supposed to be. Johann Ekk's forefathers had come from Prussia at the invitation of Catherine the Great to plow the steppes and civilize the South. The immigrants had been most eager to make the six to eight-week trek in covered wagons from the shores of the Vistula to the shores of the Dniepr since Catherine the Great had promised cheap land and eternal freedom. The faithful had come by the thousands in search for that eternal freedom, which seemed to forever elude them in Prussia. For a century they had been forced to eke out a living as laborers and craftsmen, never being able to realize what they perceived to be their God-given calling: tilling the land to enhance the goodness of the earth. In Russia, they had blossomed as farmers—their calling—but now Johann Ekk feared for his country.

Czar Nicholas II, an ineffective monarch ruling more from a base of title than aptitude, was deposed by fanatics in October of 1917. Alexander Kerensky, the young and brilliant leader of the revolution, promised a popular vote soon to determine the country's future leadership; however, before this would come to pass, the Bolchevists deposed Kerensky, forcing him to flee. Lenin, the new leader, quickly molded a firm political grip, cementing it with threats, intimidations, arrests, imprisonments, deportations, and merciless killings.

The Czar, his Czarina Alexandra, and their children, at first hoping for exile in England, were now deported to Siberia where they were held in a small basement room and murdered in cold blood the next year. Lenin's Red Party members, the Communists, where challenged by the White Party of Czarists, giving way to what appeared an endless teeter-totter war of advances and retreats, conquests and defeats, shouts of victory, and groans of death. Cities and regions changed control many times over in short periods of time and its populace, driven by blind fear for life, was forced to show allegiance, giving food, horses, wagons, and supplies to whoever happened to be in control. The state of constant conflict was seized upon by lawless bands plundering the country in search of loot and the satisfaction of the animal instinct of conquest by power.

It was now 1919, two years since the beginning of the revolution, but it seemed that the bands of Tatars and Machnos were propelled to ever growing numbers by past conquests of innocent villagers and intense rivalry among themselves.

Thus far, Rosenthal had been spared, but there were plenty of stories telling of atrocities done to the villages on the outlying northern boundaries of the settlement. Aaron Tilitzki, his protégée, friend, and long time business partner, had written from his post in Odessa in the South that things were getting increasingly difficult. In fact, the import/export business he conducted in partnership with Ekk seemed to encounter increasing numbers of obstacles. First, it had been more severe taxes, then it had been unexplained delays of shipments, then it had been the disappearance of goods without trace, and most recently, Aaron had been accused by the powers in Odessa of being unpatriotic for importing so many foreign goods.

"The Motherland can fend for itself, it has all it needs; there is no need to import what others have made, and it takes away jobs from our own people."

Neither Ekk nor Tilitzki knew the exact meaning, but both suspected a larger message behind the robbery of Aaron's warehouse a short while ago. Johann knew that they would have to do some very serious thinking and planning when Aaron next came.

Aaron did come again, for the last time, in early 1920. There was an air of uneasiness. Johann knew that the political climate was very unfavorable to business, especially the visible import/export business. He knew that this had put Aaron in a very compromising situation and that they had to make some plans both to save the business, but more importantly, to save Aaron. Marta, too, was uneasy. She had heard rumors of turmoil everywhere she went. In school she had to take classes in Communist doctrine, the religion classes were no longer taught, and the teachers seemed hesitant, even afraid. She had heard from her father that the business was facing unprecedented challenges, and that these challenges involved Aaron. Aaron?

"Marta, Aaron is coming tomorrow."

"I know." She knew because she had checked her father's calendar in the office.

"Are you glad?"

She was not sure how to answer the question. But somehow, Father's voice revealed an understanding that gave her assurance. It was okay to be glad.

No doubt, she was glad, even excited about his return, and when he did come, she received the usual proper embrace and a book. She wanted to know what the future held for Aaron, whether she would see him again, when, and how.

It occurred to her that she had never really known anything about his personal life. Was he single, married? Did he have a wife, a family? Had they died? Whatever the case, she did feel a very special bonding.

At the dinner table, the conversation between Aaron and Johann was subdued; it drifted from happenings on the estate to events in Odessa to business prospects.

"Marta, how is school, and the piano?"

"School's different. The teachers seem scared, like they don't teach what they want to teach."

Marta was happy to talk. She could look at him while she did so.

"And the piano? I hear that Olga came again?"

"Yeah, it was great. She has so many ideas."

"I suppose the lake is frozen and you spend lots of time skating?"

"It is fun."

15

"I imagine, now that it is winter, everybody is busy repairing machinery and harnesses?" Aaron turned this question to Johann.

It was small talk, which, truthfully, was not even of interest to Aaron, even though he did ask the question.

"Aaron, did you look into market possibilities for vinegar?"

"Yes, I think there are good possibilities. You probably would not even have to go much beyond Odessa itself. That market alone could be huge."

Positive statements and windows of opportunities always had the effect of fueling Johann's creativity, causing him to think broadly and in global terms.

"I'd like to pursue the vinegar business. But Aaron, you know some years ago we had lots of silkworms and produced some of the finest silk. I have been thinking about reviving that industry. What do you think?"

"Oh, I don't know. Maybe."

Johann thought that Aaron's responses were unusually subdued. Normally the two had stimulated each other's creativity. They had always complemented each other's talents—Johann in production, Aaron in marketing. Obviously now Aaron had other things in mind. Marta noticed the worrisome atmosphere.

"How are things in Odessa?" Johann decided to give Aaron a chance.

"Not so good." Aaron said, shrugging. He made the decision to talk about it, even though normally they would have retreated to the study after dinner to talk about weighty matters. He did so because he wanted Marta to be included.

"Johann, Marta, listen… bands attacked my storehouse again."

Just the fact that Aaron called each of them by name immediately signaled to Marta the ominous nature of the events. She sensed that whatever else was to come was not good.

Johann's first thought was to carry through what he had thought about for some time, namely transferring his marketing station from Odessa to Zaparozhye. This obviously would not be so favorable a site; it was much smaller, it was not as ideally suited for import/export, and it did not have the established market. However, it would certainly be closer for personal control, and it would be safer— at least for now.

But then Johann found himself embarrassed about the thought. How could his mind have gone first to the business? His friend Aaron was in danger. He should help him, of course.

"Not only that, but they also tried to burn my house. And I received several threats on my life. I don't think Odessa is safe for me anymore."

Aaron had waited to see if either would respond to his first statement, but both were quietly pursuing their own thoughts, weighing the impact of what he had said, and what it might mean for each. Johann chose to speak first and come to the bottom line.

"How can I help?"

Johann was serious. He now became genuinely concerned for his protégée, friend, and colleague.

"I won't even go back to Odessa. I have sold some of the inventory and just let the rest go. I already packed my personal belongings and had them shipped to Moscow. From here I am going to take the train to Moscow tomorrow where my luggage should be by that time.

"What will you do in Moscow?"

Marta surprised herself with her boldness, but the question came from the heart.

"I've decided to migrate to Canada. I have relatives there, you know, and I have always thought it would be interesting to explore new horizons. The turn of events here in our Motherland gives me the needed push to do what I have wanted to do for a long time, but never really had good reason to do."

The dining room was very quiet. All knew that their lives would be changed forever.

4

Aaron and Johann retreated to the study. Marta stayed behind in the dining room and she was glad to see that the door to the study was left ajar and that Aaron's profile was clearly visible as they spoke. She pretended to busy herself in the dining room, but her main thought was to watch Aaron. He was dashing, well groomed, and so proper. His hair was always in place, his clothing immaculate, in demeanor cultured. She liked the air of determination she had always noticed about him. He knew what he wanted, and how to get it.

It was later that evening when each had retreated to their own rooms. Marta could not sleep. It was hard to sort out the meaning of all the feelings coming to her in virgin form. Never had she experienced such strange attraction coupled with such sadness. She waited and prayed, not knowing for what. The anxiety built and now she could bear it no longer. She put on her warm nightgown and on quick and quiet feet, slipped into the library just before midnight. It was dark, as usual, but the cold night sky was lit up with a nearly full moon, giving the library the benefit of some of its light. She lit the kerosene lamp on the piano and looked for some music. Her father would not find it odd to hear some music; he was used to it. The chords of Beethoven's Sonata in C Sharp Minor, *The Moonlight Sonata*, came with surprising ease. Of course, she had played it many times before, and now she could enjoy the luxury of not having to pay such close attention to the fingering, the technique, the intonations, volume changes. Instead, she could enjoy it, feel it, and allow it to carry her.

Then suddenly, she sensed his presence. Even after she stopped playing she could hear nothing, but she knew he was there, somewhere in the room.

"Hello."

It was the familiar low voice. His greeting gave her freedom to turn around and see him standing in the doorway.

"What is it, Marta?"

"I don't know."

Her reply was honest.

"How was school today?"

"Really awful. I couldn't concentrate. I worried."

At this point, she didn't care how far she revealed her feelings. Aaron had moved into the room, and, without knowing what propelled her, she ran out of the room and into the kitchen, only to return a moment later.

"Have you eaten?" she asked, as she held out a cookie to him. Of course, she knew that he had eaten, but she thought perhaps the question would not sound as silly as it did if he was used to a bedtime snack.

"Shall I get you some milk?"

"You don't have to do this," he replied.

"Yes, I do... I mean, I want to... I mean, it's okay, I don't mind. I like to."

He took the cookie from her, laid it on the coffee table, and walked to the window looking at the beautiful, moonlit country.

"What is it, Marta?" he said, still facing away.

"Are you really leaving?"

"I have to; it is not safe here for me anymore. I am a business man."

She thought it was strange. How could he cut himself off from their lives and the land of his hopes? Canada was so far off.

"Here, I want you to have this."

He took something out of his coat pocket and gave it to her. She took the small wooden vase, so typical of the Russian crafts, and held it in her hands, slowly rotating its delicate form. It appeared rather light, even compared to its size. Its lid fit perfectly into the grooves carved into the lip of the vase. What intrigued Marta most was the decoration. Except for its foot, the entire vase was a black background onto which leaves, fruits, and abstract designs were painted in reds, golds, and greens. All colors were intense, almost stark. The foot and the interior of the vase were enameled in simple gold. It was beautiful.

"My mother got it from her mother, and in her later years she gave it to me. Keep it, treasure it, and allow it to hold something special you want to keep."

The lake lay forgotten in its frozen solitude, its shape clearly outlined by the moonlight from on high. She could not think of what to say or do.

"I will treasure it forever. Thank you."

"We'd better go."

"Will I see you again?"

Aaron, twice her senior, had now moved from friend to something else in her young life. Was this first love she felt?

"I will see you in the morning before I go to the train station." He meant to encourage her to leave, and she finally did move toward the door. But then, she did not. She turned, stood, and waited.

"Marta, let me tell you something."

Now his voice sounded like a father giving advice. She was not sure if she liked it.

"You are experiencing, maybe for the first time, the most beautiful part of life. You are young, intelligent, attractive, cultured, and many more such beautiful moments will come your way. Keep your chin high, and life will be a blessing for you."

"Will I see you again?" She knew there was no sure answer.

"Just concentrate on pursuing those beautiful moments in life, which you deserve so very richly.

"Look at the stars: life will bring as many blessings as you see stars. I'll see you in the morning."

She wondered what all that really meant.

5

During the next year or so, Johann busied himself in re-establishing his business. He was not a quitter. It was part of his make-up to forge ahead. It had been his grandfather who started the estate with a small flock of sheep and by selling farm products from a humble cart he had pushed to the village market. The quality of the vegetables and fruits, and the ease with which he interacted with people, the obvious drive to please, all had earned him the admiration of his neighbors, and had paid off handsomely in financial gain. That same work ethic had been passed on to his son, and in turn, to Johann.

After the traditional schooling available in the settlement, his father had sent him to Germany to study farm techniques. The two years in the agricultural school were an immersion into the latest the world had to offer in agricultural techniques, machinery, and business. But his keen mind was quick to capitalize on opportunities in all areas of life available for the asking, either in school or in the city. He knew that a sound education not only brought comfort to life, enhancing self-confidence and raising one's economic status, but it also assured that in old age, the trained and agile mind becomes a person's entertainer.

So, he participated in sports and became aware of the Roman dictum, "Healthy mind in healthy body." He read widely, purchased books, and went to lectures. He was introduced to the wonderful world of culture, literature, and music, which nourished the mind and cleared it from the cobwebs of daily toil. Social institutions were intriguing to him, since they provided a means of serving fellow human beings, and at the same time reward the creators of such institutions with profits. His vision for what was possible literally exploded with ideas. He had come home a man full of restless plans, with visions well beyond those of fellow farmers.

Johann began building his own empire on the shoulders of the success of his forefathers. Strengthened by the silent support of previous generations and the absence of significant failures, he attacked life with the vigor and confidence of a young lion. His natural and acquired tools served him well: he was meticulous, careful

21

in record keeping, willingly embraced inevitable change, and had an uncanny sense for economic trends. His predictions were on target with almost frightening frequency. He had mastered the art of human relations and was blessed with smooth politics in dealing with his fellow man, though most of lesser mind and shorter vision.

Johann built his farm in careful steps, and the estate soon became a model not only for his fellow farmers, but for most of Crimea. He built a two-story home—unheard of in the region. Instead of the traditional thatched roof or wooden shingles, he adorned his home with red cement tiles. Along the street, he set a fence in brick and forged iron—the talk of the villages. His wife was aided in her reign with a fleet of maids and servants, each assigned to specific duties.

He followed the Odessa stock market to aid in his decision-making, he published an agricultural newsletter for his fellow farmers, introduced crop rotation, the use of manure as fertilizer, he imported harvesters, and obtained advice from government agricultural agencies in Odessa. He became convinced that vegetation affected the weather and, to test the theory, he planted 10,000 trees in an experimental nursery. Soon he became the chair of the Agricultural Society, proposed an agricultural school for boys, and was sought after for counsel and advice. He encouraged teachers, and sponsored the first teacher's conferences. It would not be long until he planted mulberry trees to introduce the silk industry, experimented with vineyards, fish ponds, built his own brickyard, and started insurance and welfare systems.

An empire was being built and was thriving. But political changes kept clouding the horizon, the magnitude of which was beyond even Johann's very capable administration. More and more stories of Machno bands plundering the villages kept putting dampers on the implementation of large undertakings. After Aaron's departure, Johann had made some contacts in Zaparozhye, and for a while it did look promising, but he knew that he had to proceed with extreme caution. His entrepreneurial spirit was being confined, its wings clipped.

Once Marta had finished the available schooling, she stayed home busying herself with reading, piano, and her favorite outdoor activities: skating in the winter, and her team of horses Kukla and Mishka during the rest of the year. She thought about Aaron a lot. They had heard through others that, after many months of waiting in Moscow, he did indeed obtain the necessary documentation to emigrate. As far as she knew, he was now gone to the land of his hopes. Would she ever hear from him again? See him again? But time is a wonderful healer, especially in the young, who, through vigor and vitality, are able to suppress the surfacing of deep longings. One year, then two would pass, and with the passing of time was coupled the passing of the conscious presence of Aaron, even though that first young experience of attachment, and his parting words would remain engraved in her mind forever.

6

The winter of 1922 was cold and severe, freezing the earth to its core. Work on the land ceased, animals were kept inside, and the farm help busied itself with repairing harnesses, rebuilding the barn interior for ever more efficient flow of chores, and fashioning furniture for domestic and business needs.

The rains that had not come during the previous spring, the drought, and the inevitable crop failure that followed had given many anxious pauses. This pattern was to repeat itself the next few years and soon the small farmers began to suffer. Couple this with the Machno bands marauding through the villages and taking what they found and you would eventually get famine, and the abandoning of the farms and the emigration of most of the population. But that was few years down the road—a future no one could see, and few imagined. But now it was winter, a time to skate.

Marta loved this time of year. It gave her freedom to skate on the smooth pond below the farm. Throughout the cold days, people, young and old, came to the pond either across the land or skating up the canal from their respective farms. This pond had the reputation of particularly clean and smooth ice, and it belonged to an inviting host; coming to skate here was easy. In the evenings the crowds would swell to larger numbers, when indulgence in entertainment would not be looked upon askance in a community where high work ethic was worshipped as though a religious ritual.

It was quite obvious that Marta was by far the best skater. No wonder, for she did have all that free time to skate. But more than the hours of practice, her seventeen-year-old athletic body was endowed with coordinated movements and a grace that were brought out nowhere else more shiningly than in skating. She seemed to float above the ice. The forward movement of one foot was translated as a wave traveling up her body and repeated with the forward motion of the next foot. There seemed to be a symphonic synergy between the movements of her feet and the rest of her body. One encouraged the other. The beauty of a body in motion could not be better expressed, even when that body was covered with heavy dark shawls and skirts of great expanse—the expected attire for women. Men had the advantage of wearing pants, which allowed them to move their legs with much less restriction. Still, within that upside-down-umbrella hiding her lower body, there was carefree motion, which the large skirt had no choice but to follow and translate to the outside. Her practiced movements were freed from any necessary concentration. She was free to talk with others, gaze into the far distance, and propel herself with great speed. She loved speed. She seemed to be driven by a secret force. It looked so easy and effortless as her perfectly straight and erect body sliced through the winter air, her long blond hair flagging behind.

It was during these evening community skating events that she first noticed him. She noticed him not so much because he was a young man, but because he, too, was an excellent skater who seemed to love speed. At times, their paths would cross; at times, they skated parallel to each other going in the same or, at other times, in opposite directions. His clothing described a poor worker, who obviously just came from a barn somewhere. She did not remember seeing him before. Not even in church. His skates had old fashioned, semi-homemade wooden frames, which were tied onto his working boots—nothing like her white, imported skates with shiny steel blades. But he did not seem to mind his clearly low cast standing; instead, he displayed a happy smile and a carefree interaction with those around him. He, too, was quick to notice the other good skater in the crowd.

"Want to race?" he asked her as they skated past each other, staying just long enough in hearing proximity. She did not answer, pretending not to hear, but chose to keep a careful watch on his maneuvers. Soon they were close enough again, but instead of asking, he challenged:

"I'll beat you to the other side."

That was the direction she was going already, and a continuance of that direction could not necessarily be construed as a positive response to his challenge. Once at the opposite side of the pond, they turned about and, without speaking, crossed the large pond again; then began to circle it with ever increasing speed.

"What's your name?" she wanted to know, as they flew past other, slower skaters.

"Peter. Peter Voran. And yours?"

"I am Marta. I live here."

"Ah, you're Mr. Ekk's daughter."

"Yes. Where are you from?"

It was not easy for Peter to talk about his standing in society. Had it not been for his happy and carefree approach to life, his lot in life could have easily been cause for despair. But he knew from experience that his ready smile and willing disposition toward others had overshadowed his "nobody" position in the community. That, he knew instinctively, would serve him better than anything else he knew.

It was not his fault that he was born into a family without land, and therefore without voting rights and without stature. They had always lived at the end of villages where his father had been a craftsman for the landowners and his mother had hired herself out as household help. Growing up he had learned to respect the people who were landowners—those who had farms. To them it did not make much difference whether people were small time farmers or owners of large estates. A landowner was somebody. They were the ones that sat up front in church services, they made the decisions for the community, and they were the ones who had the large weddings. Peter had learned from the way his mother and father talked about "Mrs. Boldt" and "Mr. Reimer," and all the other rich people they had worked for, that these were special people, people that would never come to their house, except to leave something to be fixed. In fact, Peter had been told that you did not just go up and down the village street where the stately homes with ornate railing fences and pretty gardens were. You only walked into the village when you had business there.

Peter and his parents had moved often in search of work, always retreating to the lowly housing at the end of the village. Given the scarcity of farmland, the large families, and the strict rules of inheritance, it was virtually impossible for them to expect release from this bondage. Uneducated, they remained dependent; the small crumbs of life became their victories. His father found solace in playing his harmonica, which gave him and his family endless enjoyment and comfort during the evening hours. He had only been thirty-eight years of age when he contracted that dreaded influenza, which in the absence of access to medical care had swiftly claimed his life. Now it was Peter who, as the eldest child, found work in Rosenthal with small-time farmer David Dueck not too far from the end of the village. At eighteen, he had been exposed to all kinds of work, and being a farmhand was not new. They were given a cottage at the end of the village to live in and his mother had quickly found work by not asking for high wages.

Peter did not feel like answering Marta's question, but she seemed genuinely interested.

"We just moved here." He left it at that.

Marta was mesmerized. From then on, she went skating every evening, hoping to see him again. He did not come until three days later when she immediately recognized him. Of course, she noticed his carefree skating style, but she let her eyes feast on that tall muscular frame of his. His dark hair had a wild nature about it. It certainly was not cared for often; parted in the middle it hung freely to either side, but that gave it the looks of beastly beauty. His square jaw told of a strong manhood, his dimpled smile of a happy spirit.

"Hi."

"Hi, how are you?" It was a safe question for her to ask.

"Fine. Want to skate around the pond?"

"Okay."

They seemed to skate often, meeting through accidental but planned encounters. They enjoyed the physical exercise—on a few occasions they had even held hands in the prescribed manner for couples' skating—but even more than that, they enjoyed the feeling all these activities created between them.

7

David Dueck was a demanding boss to work for. Being a citizen with moderate means springing from his small farm, he was driven by the urge to better himself financially and maybe someday become a large-scale farmer. During the monthly assembly meetings where the male heads of village landowners decided on community issues, David Dueck felt challenged to do more and better as he saw the large landowners do. He was at times intimidated by the loud talk of these fat cats, who, encouraged by their material successes, obviously loved to hear themselves talk during these public meetings. These confused emotional messages David Dueck carried secretly within translated their high demands onto his hired help. Everyday, Peter had to work long hours. Even though religious tradition absolutely forbade any type of work on Sundays, the care for animals was exempted. Thus, Peter found himself working seven days a week and it would be a long time before he would enjoy even a single day of vacation.

Early in the morning, he arrived on the Dueck farm to feed the horses, after which he joined the other help in the worker kitchen for breakfast. He usually spent all day in the fields; in fact, to save time lunch was usually brought to the fields, allowing the men to rest for twenty minutes. Even during a rain the work continued, unless it became a torrential downpour converting the rich earth into heavy mud. Even after supper was finished, he still had to go back to the barn to feed the horses again.

Most everybody had to work with the manure, especially in the winter when the animals were kept inside the barns. It was a backbreaking job to haul the stinking mass in huge wheelbarrows from the barns to the backyard. Here the refuse was processed eventually to become a household fuel, the only available fuel in this wood-barren land. Nothing was wasted. The pile grew longer and wider and taller to eventually fill the wooden form measuring six feet tall and fifteen by fifteen at the base. While to the casual eye this was a mere pile, to those whose stretched muscles and strained backs had labored to bring about its size from the never-ending supply, this was a huge mountain.

Throughout the winter the mountain lay dormant, but with the first touch of warmth from the earliest days of spring, the mountain became a monster, alive with warm ferment moving within, and a million flies buzzing without. It was now time to cut off the rotted outside layer on all sides and spread that layer as fertilizer into the fields prior to spring plowing. The now freshly peeled, strongly reeking matter was spread flat to a depth of a foot and kneaded for hours with horses' hoofs doing the monotonous work. The greenish mass was then allowed to dry for several days in the spring sun so as to become a clay-like paste. It was back-breaking to now cut one-foot cube pieces, set them on end to dry some more, and then turn them a few times end-for-end to continue the drying process. Once crispy dry, the cherished fuel cubes were stored for use.

It was on one of those long days, when the mountain refused to get smaller and the just-finished lunch lay heavy in the stomach that Peter lay down on a board trying to rest his burdened bones. David Dueck found him and gave him a simple warning.

"We don't sleep at this place."

It was strict. Peter knew that Mr. Dueck lay down for a nap virtually every noon, and always did the easy work around the farm, and often even that was not physical work at all. It was clear to Peter that Mr. Dueck was the boss, but why should all the extra heavy work go to the lowliest workers?

It was the next Sunday at the worship services that he saw her again. He had cleaned up right after chores and managed to get to church just a few minutes late. His usual place in the back of the building was still available. As he sat down, he looked around and found her sitting way up front with her father. The familiar songs were sung in the slow, harmonious tones he had heard since childhood, and the preaching was the same long routine mouthing words he also had heard, so it seemed, since he was a toddler. After the service, he lingered about the entrance, and when she came out she slowed down upon eyeing him. Her father had stopped earlier to talk with others. Peter moved closer.

"Hi, how are you?" he asked, his voice barely above a whisper and his eyes slightly averted from her face.

"Fine."

"Can I see you sometime soon?"

Spotting her father turning toward her, she smiled briefly. "I don't know. I'll see. I have to go."

Still, they managed to arrange occasional encounters. After the winter months had converted the glassy pond surface to a splashy playground for ducks and geese, Marta had her well-fed Kukla and Mishka hitched up to the buggy to ride about the village. It was an elegant sight to behold: two dark horses with gleaming coats covering a myriad of ready muscles, whose anxious vitality was translated into a high-tailed, curved-necked ride announced by the sharp clicks of the octet of hoofs. While it was understood from past trips that she was out simply for a joy ride—perhaps to visit girlfriends—and to the unsuspecting eye, nothing had changed, her destiny had now become sharply focused. She was searching for ways to meet Peter; and since the interest was mutual, the search was soon successful and quickly became an elaborately engineered routine arrangement.

She stopped the team behind the little house, out of street sight, and knocked on his door.

"I can't stay long. I just came to say hi." She was actually proud of her boldness in seeking him out.

"Can I come to see you at your house?" It was a question he had to ask.

"That won't work, because Father will not permit it."

"I know, I know. You are high society."

The pain of that reality was equally intense for both of them. Both had known that this would eventually come up, and both knew that there really was no solution to this centuries-old unwritten social code: casts do not intermingle, especially not from such extreme opposites.

Unexpectedly, Peter found himself one day with a legitimate reason to appear at the front door of the Ekk estate. David Dueck, who was applying for a short-term loan, had written out the request, as required by the loan committee run by the local cooperative and chaired by Johann Ekk. But Dueck found it beneath his dignity to walk down to the Ekk estate and deliver the request. He did not like begging. It seemed to him that the system almost insisted that he beg.

The best solution was to send his cheap farmhand with the sealed envelope.

"I've got a message from Mr. Dueck," he said to Natasha, who appeared to answer the knock on the door. She would have taken the envelope for later delivery, but Johann Ekk entered the foyer and received it from Peter.

"Aren't you Peter...?"

"Peter Voran, yes sir."

"Yeah, I heard about you. Well, tell Mr. Dueck we'll let him know."

As Peter turned, he got a glimpse of Marta at the top of the stairs who had heard his voice and could not contain her curiosity, yet found herself restrained by her father's presence. What did Father mean by, "I heard about you?" Did he know? Had he simply heard that he had moved to Rosenthal recently, and now worked for Mr. Dueck? The tension between expected rejection of the blossoming relationship, and the powerful attraction the two youth felt, manifested itself as excruciating pain, yet that very pain seemed to give strength to their determination to see each other.

Some time ago, she had given up the disciplined piano practices. She hoped that Father would take this to be so because Olga had, after all those years, given notice that she no longer could make those long trips. Several times, she had left her invitation for Marta to come to see her in Zaparozhye to play the piano and go to concerts. A first visit had yet to materialize. She could feel her whole being caught on a one-way road in search of fulfillment, which she was determined to find no matter what.

They had managed to find a time to be together at Peter's two-room hut. His mother was away putting in her long hours as a household help. Marta had once again driven her team down to the village to explore. She felt that the feelings boiling inside her were about to explode and needed a resolve, and that today she would let nature take its course. He had not even tried to kiss her yet. She did get the distinct feeling that he might be afraid, since he thought she was so much better than he. He had kept his distance. It was flattering and it was frustrating.

After tying up the team behind the house, she entered the tiny room. He came up to her and held her, though he was always careful. It felt so good. In his own crude way, he was always a gentleman and that just piqued her curiosity. What would he be like when he let go of his inhibitions?

They sat down on the small wooden bench and Marta felt butterflies in her stomach. Peter touched her hair, very carefully, then her cheeks, and now moved his fingers just past her lips.

"You are beautiful," he said.

He took her hand and clasped it firmly into his, then folded their clasped hands around her waist.

She remained quiet, feverishly processing feelings and anticipating the immediate future. They sat there for what appeared to be a long time, but then he put his arms around her and kissed her. His sealed lips held that kiss until he could feel her body relax and give itself to destiny, then he opened his lips and kissed her again. She opened hers and the two tongues began a dance of joy, flooding their bodies with emotions. Is this what Aaron had meant by the blessing of life she was to receive so bountifully? she wondered. It was good to be alive.

His right hand fell from her shoulder onto her chest, which was well hidden by her coat. Her heartbeat seemed to choke her breath. She wanted to stop him, and then she was afraid he would stop. His hot, quick breath was on her neck, and she wondered if she should make some kind of move. She knew this was going too far and they must stop, but the wave of new sensations paralyzed her. After all, what could really happen to her virtue on this rigid, hard bench? She did not want to be this excited, but then she felt that she wanted to lie down.

"I must go." She said it not so much out of desire as of fear. Would her father miss her? Had she been gone too long?

"When can I see you again?"

"I don't know." And with that she was out the door, onto the buggy, and out of the yard.

Peter heard the hard gallop lose itself in the distance.

8

"We received a letter from Aaron." Father was happy and wanted to share his joy with someone.

"Oh? What does he say?" She was excited. Quick as lightening her feelings flashed back from the excitement she now enjoyed, to the first attachment she had felt some years ago.

"He seems to have arrived in good shape and is beginning his work in Canada. He lives in Toronto, but is preparing to move to Winnipeg."

Father was obviously excited to have heard from his friend, and he seemed genuinely glad for him that he could find new beginnings. He gave the letter to Marta. She sat on the lower steps of the stairs going up to the second story and read. She was transported back to another time—it appeared an almost ancient time. As she read, she thought of the new awakening she had felt her body go through, the special attraction she had felt for Aaron, and the good conversations they had had.

Aaron's letter had asked about her, how she was doing, what her plans were. She did not really feel like writing to him. This was a different time. Aaron had been gone a long time. She was in love—again—now with Peter, who was younger, perhaps wilder, rougher, and more down to earth. She just wished her father would accept him even though he was from the other side of the tracks. She had to find a way to see him again.

The opportunity presented itself when the church-sponsored youth picnic was announced. A series of wagons were to take the village young people miles out of the village onto a park-like pasture near the Dniepr. Marta rode with the girls and there were several wagons of them. She knew that Peter would also go and expected him to be on the wagons ahead of hers.

It was not long after arrival that she saw him. They talked and decided to get away after some time with the group. It was barely a half hour when they walked toward the woods, and as soon as they had turned the corner around the bushes, he again clasped her hand into his and put the clasped hands around her waist. She liked that. It felt grown up.

They came to a clearing, and in the middle of it was an old, abandoned hut. They circled the hut and found a beautiful meadow dotted with a few trees just on the other side of the hut. Peter pulled on the clasped hands and impulsively moved her toward him, embracing her hard. He held her close and long, and she felt his awakening manhood. He moved away just a bit to save both of them embarrassment. He noticed that she had her arms around his back and her head on his shoulder. He lifted her head and kissed her again and again, exploring the innocent young freshness of her mouth.

In dazzled ecstasy, she felt herself being lifted and carried into a wonderland. She snuggled her face into the warmth of his neck and wishing she could stay there always in this lovely, secure place. They were now laying down on the meadow, entwined in what seemed an everlasting kiss. She closed her eyes, trying to feel all the power of that sweet plunder of his lips.

His hands were all over her body. She thought of objecting, then accepted it, then simply enjoyed it. He stroked her skin in safe places. He kissed her intensely and it all combined to give her an obscene excitement.

Then she heard a groan, quickly realizing that it was her own throat giving audible expression to inner joy—but by now she did not care anymore. The one-way road on which her feelings had catapulted her was reaching the needed destiny of resolution. She had read about the sudden convergence of feelings exploding within the body, like sneezing. Would she experience it? Would he? She expected him to make another move, but he did not. She realized that he wanted her to feel the power, the beauty, and the excitement of this pleasure. He was gentle, retreating when needed, but persistent in his pursuit to have her experience what joy there can be. He seemed so experienced. Peter's fingers gave birth to ever new sensations, heretofore never experienced, and she thought if he stopped she would explode. She allowed herself to be molded by his overtures, to be melted away into a sea of gently rocking pleasure.

Suddenly a dog barked and Marta jumped. Her lips were sore and she felt strange. Would he still like her?

"Ek see di goat." I love you. He said it from the heart as the Low German he used came from the depth of his people's soul. She breathed deeply and with relief.

They stood now. He embraced her and told her again that he loved her.

"Do you think you can love me?"

Her head, now lying on his huge chest, nodded lightly.

"Can I see you soon?" he asked.

"Okay."

As they walked back to the picnic, they knew that that day their lives fused emotionally.

9

"I want you to stop seeing him." It was not very often that her father used such a loud voice and harsh tones. Even the volume and intensity could not hide the quivers of anger in his voice.

"I love him, and I want to see him."

"No. Do you know what you are getting yourself into? Do you know who he is? Do you know what kind of life you would have with him? His father was never able to provide for his kin, and this fellow is from the same stock."

"He has a name. His name is Peter—Peter Voran. And I love him. You cannot stop me from seeing him."

She and her father had not often quarreled. Johann had always taken a protective attitude toward her. She was the only one still home; she was the only surviving daughter; she was gentle in spirit; quick in mind; and accommodating to the wishes of her father, whom she revered greatly. Johann wanted the best for her—of course. He could provide anything for her that she wanted, or that he wanted for her. In his mind, the ideal would be that she would meet someone of her stature, someone with a land inheritance to come, someone who knew the ins and outs of big time farming, of running an estate. Perhaps that someone could eventually even take over the Ekk estate. Johann had often thought about various possibilities. If Abraham, his oldest and only surviving son, became established enough on his own, then all that needed to be done was to make sure an equitable estate settlement between the two was carried out. On the other hand, if Marta would not get married to someone capable—or not get married at all—then other arrangements would obviously have to be made.

But Johann had not been quite prepared for this kind of possibility. Why would Marta stoop so low, to become involved with someone without means, without experience, without drive? Someone like Peter would certainly only be a parasite, living off the estate, likely giving up whatever work habits he had acquired to entertain himself with his father's harmonica.

All of this was particularly troubling given the political uncertainty the country was in. Now more then ever, Johann needed

36

help to carefully plan for an uncertain future. It had been some five years now since the Bolshevik revolution and there did not seem any sort of political stability in the making. In fact, unrest seemed to come closer and closer to their remote settlements. Why, just a few weeks ago there had been rumors of lawless bands again raiding some of the outlying villages, stealing horses, demanding food, taking grain and wagons, and harassing the inhabitants. It was clear to him what this might eventually lead to. The pattern was familiar from what was happening further north where the Red and White armies traded dominance of villages, cities, and entire regions. Their see-saw back and forth switching of control was interrupted only by the terrorizing bands wildly riding through the nights for quick plunder and rich spoil. Their law was the mood of the moment, their enforcement of that law the sword in the hand and the gun in the holster.

It was evident to Johann that it was this lawlessness that had caused the lean times up north where people had abandoned the land, even the ready harvest. Or, where the harvest had been gathered, it had to be handed over to demanding daredevils in the hope of thereby trading one's life. Famine was imminent. Undernourished bodies became vulnerable to attack—both physical and biological—and once famine and plagues obtained a foothold, their ravaging sweep across the land knew no boundaries. Johann saw the advance of this unseen threat, and soon it might reach their own peaceful villages. His fears would come to fruition all too soon.

Marta's thoughts were on other matters—matters of the heart. Her young body had matured, now demanding the experience that belongs to youth. The throbbing encounters with Peter had catalyzed something new to her being, awakening within her ever sweeter sensations crying for desperate fulfillment—whatever the costs. No social code could keep them apart. It would have taken steel shackles and stone prisons to separate what nature united.

Their secret encounter was in the barn on the estate where Marta naturally spent time tending her beloved horses. Risking his job and a possible violent encounter with Johann Ekk, Peter frequently escaped from home and duty to see Marta.

Tonight Father was away on business, the farmhands had done their chores, and Marta walked outside knowing that Peter would soon show up. And she was not disappointed. His tall frame appeared from the garden where he had chosen to walk to avoid discovery.

"Hi," he whispered.

Her insides jumped with excitement.

"Hi. You want to go see the horses?" The minute she said it, she thought that certainly it was too brash a move. He would think she was too pushy. After all, it was in the barn that a lot of things did happen—or so she had heard.

"Sure." He said it so matter of factly. But she wondered if perhaps he, too, was nervous with anticipation of the unknown. Walking across the orchard, he suddenly took her hand. It felt reassuring. She liked the way he made her feel good about her sexuality. She squeezed it, giving the signal that she agreed.

They stood in the small hay chamber separated from the horse stalls by a low fence so that the hay could easily be thrown over to feed the horses. A pitchfork was leaning into the corner. Everything looked clean and taken care of. It appeared that the world was as it should be. Each horse in its stall, content with feed and rest. Even the odor spoke of a freshly cleaned barn.

She leaned over the fence to look at the horses. Rather than standing next to her, Peter stood behind her, leaning heavily against her and putting his arms around her. Her heart catapulted and she was sure that his strong arms around her could feel the enormous pounding of her heart against her chest. Again, she wondered what she was to do next. But then, she didn't care, really. She wouldn't care if she were found out. She wouldn't worry about consequences, not now.

She could feel his breath on the back of her neck. He started to kiss her neck. It was so romantic and arousing. She had read about sex, but wondered what it was really like. Reading about it and doing it could not be the same.

Then he turned her around, holding her tight and pushing her body against the railing. He kissed her, almost violently, and thrust his tongue deep into her mouth. She answered gleefully by responding in like manner, as she felt him pressing against her. She was shy—he knew that. Should she make a move to break the mood, defuse the course of events now so clearly advancing? She looked at his handsome face, the face she dreamed about so often. It was now so close to hers. *Please love me, love me forever,* she thought. No, she would not lose a chance to make that face wholly hers, to possess it forever.

How? They did not know. Why? They did not care. But somehow their knees buckled under the weight of emotions now flooding their bodies, and they found themselves lying on a bed of straw.

They emerged an hour later, exhausted and happy. Silently they walked back through the garden, but before they reached the house, Peter escaped sideways through the darkened grove.

Back in her room, Marta smiled and relived the hour just past. She thought about the power she had held over him, as she had gazed into that well-sculptured face she so adored. She saw it hypnotized with pleasure as it contorted—eyes squeezed shut, mouth open, gasping for air. And she had felt a deep and pleasurable pain! They had dissolved into each other, the one becoming the other, the two becoming one. They enjoyed the fresh salty sweat protruding from their explored bodies.

That evening their lives had fused physically.

How they did not know, but they both knew that somehow they would officially become one.

However, neither knew what great changes were awaiting them, as worlds were to tear them apart.

Riwen Forester

Part II

Love Made in Heaven

Riwen Forester

1

For once she was not running. During the last forty-five minutes or so, she had been holding on to a post on the upper deck of the *Ciudad de Buenos Aires* and staring over to the right side of the ship. Somehow, she sensed that the weeks of boat travel were over, and that it was here that a new life was to begin.

Mother Voran seemed relieved. The youngest of her brood of five, seven-year-old Hanna, had always been the liveliest and most curious. But it seemed that ever since they had reached the tropics, the warmth had given the child an extra dose of vitality. Running from side to side, up and down the many stairways, opening doors and lids, she had explored the entire ship during the first half-day. This was particularly easy for her to do on this smaller river boat they had been on since leaving the delta of the Rio de la Plata, and which was now taking them upstream into a new land. It was easier because the boat was smaller, but also because the crew and native passengers took such a delight in this active little blond bee.

She was a skinny bundle of energy whose long, golden braids waved in the air as she flew about. The fair complexion of her skin, the shiny face, the ready smile, and above all the big blue eyes were in such contrast to the dark skin, black hair, and black eyes of the native passengers. The bright tropical sun seemed to spotlight her person as she darted from place to place. The natives responded with delight to her infectious vigor and always wanted to touch her fair skin and blond hair. All who saw her smiled and felt good.

And it was hard for Mother Voran to be upset with her. After all, she had always been into things. Even since early childhood she had constantly been exploring everything, such a dynamo of delightful life; how could she be upset? She was her youngest, her sunshine, her most immediate and intimate link to her husband Peter, now laboring somewhere in the vast forests of Siberia—if not already dead. Still, she had to be watched. She seemed to know no fear, and the only time she did sit still was to eat.

But now, on this third day on the *Ciudad de Buenos Aires,* for once she stood still. An hour or so ago they had passed a big bend in the river and saw a rather lonesome mountain close to the shore. People on the ship called it "Lambaré." Like all the words in the native language, this, too, was hard to pronounce. It was supposed to be the name of an Indian chief who had resided here a long time ago. They told the story of how the *conquistadores* had battled the Indians at this site who then, after a siege of many weeks, were forced to surrender. The terms of surrender demanded that the Indians supply each of the Spanish soldiers with two young Indian women... She wondered if Indians still lived in this country.

Now the river had straightened out again, and the ship was slowly making its way into the bay that was to produce a harbor. She had watched with fascination a huge, round cupola off in the distant city. It appeared to be the dome of a large church. The haunting sounds of its great bells rolled over the city as though covering it with an invisible layer of protection. Certainly it was the tallest structure there. But what interested her more were the red tile roofs on all houses. Such roofs were new to her experience. She thought it would be like living in a fairy tale world and hoped that they, too, would have a house with red tiles. As the ship came closer, she saw many people, especially children, dressed in white. She looked at her own dark things and wondered what white would look like on her.

Life in the new city was exciting. While the grown ups worried about daily existence and making arrangements to find the proper land for their hoped-for farm life, the children were free to absorb the sights and sounds of this city in the tropics.

Much of the daily life seemed to be lived on the streets. Vendors with all kinds of wares could be seen. Fruit stands, candies, chickens bound to each other's legs, sandals, and anything else one could possibly need were available right on the street.

She could not get her eyes off the many women in long, flowing dresses that carried heavy laden baskets on their heads. They always walked so very erect and kept the basket perfectly balanced as they went from house to house to sell their goods. She noticed that when they took the basket off their heads or put them back on, people would often give them a hand to place it just right and balance it. Onto the head they first made a nest from a long piece of cloth, which was draped into a rope, then curled into a tight circle that fit the head and gave a flat surface for the basket to rest on. Some women did not just carry fruit and vegetables, but chickens, meat, coal, and many other things.

Also intriguing was the sight of market ladies riding through town on donkeys. They rode sitting sideways, protecting the goods in the big pouches hanging on either side of the donkey. As they traveled through the streets, the donkey's hoofs made a rhythmic clicking sound on the cobblestoned streets. That familiar clickity-clack became a beautiful sound, one which she could hear early in the morning before dawn when the donkeys trotted past to the market with their fresh produce.

Larger items were transported through town using two-wheeled ox or mule carts. The metal-rimmed wheels made an awesome grinding noise as they hammered through the streets. The men in these carts often drank tea from a hand-held bowl with a metal straw. It was passed from person to person and seemed to produce such a congenial atmosphere.

Not only did she discover many new and amazing things, but she herself often was a new and exciting object of admiration. Her fair skin, her very blond hair dangling about in two braids, produced joy among her dark-haired neighbors. The mummified faces of old ladies broke into toothless smiles as they reached out their petrified hands, forever wanting to touch her skin, her hair.

School children seemed to run in droves at all times during the day. They all had the same white uniform and always seemed happy, but spoke such a strange language.

These were happy weeks in the city spent leisurely while waiting to move to the country. Along with her friends, Hanna visited parks, marveled at the orange trees lining the streets, looked into many stores, admired the harp musicians, saw monuments of men on horses, and walked many streets. Although she never did get there, off in the distance she often noticed the statue of an angel way at the peak of a very high street. The statue was the culmination of a steep street with many, many steps leading up to it. It almost seemed that the steps led directly to heaven—at least the angel at the top of the tall column did point to heaven. She always wondered what it would be like there, and what the angel might look like from up close. The sight became engraved into her memory.

2

"Study, study, study. Study long and hard, son. Not only is there beauty in the discovery of knowledge, but studies also bring about security for your future. You can always find a job when you are educated! Education is one of the best investments in both time and money one can make. No one can take away an education; it stays with you always."

Ernesto had heard his father's message many times and in many different forms. The home was built around books, studies, music, and culture. Ernesto did not doubt the validity of the elder's claim; in fact, he was planning to devote a good portion of his formative years to studies. Furthermore, he did enjoy school, even though during his teen years the curriculum was strictly prescribed.

He was a youth developing quickly into a man. Long on legs and short on torso during his early teens, he had looked like someone on stilts, but now he had proportioned out. While not particularly handsome, his 6'1" slender frame, his dark brown hair, and his intensely penetrating brown eyes struck a rather imposing figure. He fit in normally into the social arena, though he was a bit shy about approaching girls who, to him, seemed always to be doing the right thing, always appearing to be courteous and proper—much like his mother and his only sister. Nevertheless, as the oldest of five, he had learned early on to take control and to be in charge.

The joys of studies came in many forms. Foreign language studies he coupled—at least in his mind—with geography and fascinating pictures of other lands and people where imaginary journeys produced sheer magic. The careful analysis and synthesis of a sentence, putting in proper place all the nouns, verbs, adverbs, adjectives, prepositions and pronouns, was as satisfying as accomplishing the assemblage of a puzzle. The discovery that the origin of many modern words lay hidden in the treasures of Greek and Latin was as exciting as opening a present. The preciseness and predictability of scientific phenomena produced amazing awe.

Mathematics was taught by Señorita Alvarez, the aging, humorless spinster who claimed her spectacles were like mirrors telling her what went on in class when she turned her face to the blackboard. Her fierce insistence on discipline gave respect both to her person and to the field she taught. It was she who taught Ernesto how to solve for x in a proportionality, and the fact that when a two-digit number, adding up to nine or less, is multiplied by eleven, the product is always the first number followed by the sum of the two, and ending with the last number—an idea he celebrated. It was she who took fifteen minutes every day to do mental drills, not only on adding and subtracting, but also multiplying, dividing, squaring, square rooting, and estimating. By calling on students randomly, she insisted that everyone participate, "In order to oil the rusty gears of your minds." She handed out rare postage stamps from all over the world as awards for accomplishment. Señorita Alvarez taught Ernesto the power of a regimented mind and will.

He was intrigued to discover the profound influence of Roman law on the modern legal system. Never had he felt such a tingling sensation in his spine as when his experienced instructor had read a poem, causing to resonate within him the chords of deep feeling. He enjoyed the literature of the great Spanish authors such as Juan Valdes, Calderon, Lope de Vega, and Garcilaso de la Vega. Cervantes' *Don Quijote* and Juan Valera's *Pepita Jiménez* were specials, which he loved to read aloud to hear the beautiful sounds of the eloquent Spanish. He spent hours with the German classics, such as Goethe's *Faust,* and memorizing Schiller's *Die Glocke.* There was no doubt Ernesto's mind was stretched, and his spirits lifted as he eagerly absorbed that which was at hand.

"Yes Ernesto, it is a simple fact of life that those who can discipline their minds will be able to control their lives, its events, its things, and ultimately even the persons who control things and events. The educated are always in charge. But it takes stern discipline to get there."

The words had the familiar high-nosed and stubborn determination that the immigrant population had inherited from its cradle in Germany, taken along during its persecution-driven wanderings to Prussia, Russia, and now to this strange Latin setting. The centuries-old hopes of peaceful and permanent settlement always seemed to give way to uprooted flight, most recently spawned by the madness of Stalin and Hitler. Still, while the people's spirit was bent, it was not broken, even though they now found themselves transplanted amidst a strange culture in this landlocked upriver country of the tropics.

It was a generous country these immigrants found themselves in. Bathed in sun and rain, its soil seemed to produce without effort. Its people, proud descendants of Indians and the heroic Spanish and Portuguese *conquistadores,* languished through the day enjoying the long, protective siestas. In the days of conquest during the early 1500s, this land had seen the valiant advances of Garcia, Juan de Salazar, founder of the river capital, and Domingo Martínez de Irala, all explorers who established a vast territory, making it the governing center of the Spanish Crown for all of South America for well over a century.

The easy life in this sleepy town produced a content, happy people wallowing through time on their hammocks. The city took daily comfort in its routine. Before dawn, the market ladies came riding down the cobblestoned street on their donkeys burdened heavily with manioc, pineapple, and health herbs. Theirs was a solitary ride in these early hours, embellished only by the ever-constant rhythmic clickity-clack of the hoofs drumming their beat onto the street.

Their destination was the city market, which seemed to have homesteaded itself, without official plan, somewhere at a convenient intersection blocking traffic in every direction. There the market lady claimed her several square feet of sidewalk, clearing it of trash and garbage, and spreading her fresh goods now at the mercy of roving dogs heading for the butcher booth and the muddy rain produced by traversing mule wagon with its wheels crashing into wet dirt pits. It was onto this happy cacophony of vegetables and garbage, meat and stray dogs, that the city's homemakers soon converged for the day's supply of necessities. Though constantly repulsed by the careless mix of food and filth, the immigrants learned to adjust.

They adjusted to cooking with coal, which they bought from the man who came down the street on Mondays shouting, *"Carbon, Carbon, Carbon..."* And to maintain freshness in these hostile tropics they learned to buy milk and fish every day.

Adjustments were expected everywhere. Their homes in Europe had been set in isolation among orchards, whereas now they found themselves sleeping in rooms with windows open to the busy sidewalks of the city. For the cleanliness-conscious matrons, the cobwebs in the high, column-studded ceilings of their houses were an invitation to do battle. The grinding sound of sand on the hard tile floor was as uncomfortable as it was new. Two-hour siestas were a must to maintain the body, yet seemed such a waste of time during the middle of the day.

But the immigrants did eventually get used to the heat, the barefoot soldiers, and the torrential downpours, which converted the streets to Venetian waterways. They learned to eat manioc instead of potatoes, tangerines instead of apples; they learned to live with all of it and even began to prosper. Their powerful Prussian pride developed an intricate cast system marking carefully designed discrimination lines between themselves and the "local" populace. The market poor, the Indians roaming the streets, and the laborers all would be dealt with only as need dictated; whereas the Spanish professionals were more accepted, and indeed often compared with or even used as models of accomplishment—yet the thought of social interaction or, heaven forbid, intermarriage with them, would be considered an infraction against God's will.

The unwritten understandings of differentiation also permeated the immigrant society itself, placing professionals, teachers, and ministers who, in addition to Spanish, readily spoke both the High and Low German, on a tall pedestal from which it was easy to cast downgrading thoughts toward those not so prepared. Such social codes, more traditional than reasonable, more self-serving than fair, were given unspoken importance, and furthermore seemed to be given the undeserved power of a religious foundation.

It was in this city of contrasts that Ernesto lived, embedded in a society within a society. As the oldest son of a professional immigrant family, he was given all the tools for the expected intellectual success. Books, music, and profound dinner discussions—ranging from the pros and cons of local community issues and sweeping changes in world politics, to the impact-laden message in Norman Vincent Peale's *The Power of Positive*

Thinking—all shaped his mind early on. Some years earlier, the family had made the difficult decision to leave the farming community and move to the capital city to provide for greater educational opportunities. Two cultures now rushed at him: The staunch Germanic emphasis on discipline, study, and success on the one hand, and the Spanish environment as the vessel for the realization of success, on the other. The challenge was to use all possible opportunities of the official educational system, yet at the same time maintain strong roots in the immigrant culture. At the helm of this ship of life was the father, who, with love and stern punishment, kept a firm hand on the straight course marked along a fine line. Strict discipline had, in Ernesto's younger days, often been emphasized with severe spankings, the expressions of Germanic love. Ernesto remembered being in the shower with his cousin and both boys counting blue spanking streaks on each other's backs. Both boys wondered how, with such harshness, their fathers could say that spankings pained them in their hearts. But it was clear that good will was the basis for all their actions.

Ernesto fondly remembered though the times when, as a little boy he rode with his father on a bike tightly hanging on to the strong waist before him. He remembered the care with which his father had watched over him as they were riding all night with a wagon load filled high with hay. To make sure the sleeping boy would not fall off into the night, Father tied him with ropes in several directions carefully explaining to him what he did. Ernesto also remembered his first exposure to astronomy, which came late one night when father and son were riding alone on a slow, horse-drawn wagon admiring the awesome display of heavenly beauty. With patience, Father taught him to recognize Orion and the Southern Cross, images now engraved in his mind forever.

At times in the evening, Ernesto would go two blocks to the north to The Angel statue where it was quiet and traffic free. He strolled about watching the ever-present love couples holding hands and kissing. Then he would sit on the low retaining wall, look at the star-filled sky above, then the city below, pondering his place in this world and wondering what the future would hold for him. In his mind's ear, he could hear the words: "Study, study long and hard, son...

Education is one of the best investments in both time and money one can make."

3

"Work, work, work. Children, that's the only way I know how we are going to survive." Mother Voran spoke to her brood not so much to educate as to vent her fears. She was alone, and burdened with responsibility for five minors in an unknown and unfriendly forest. Her early privileged life in Russia had not prepared her for this.

"You are really going to have to help, please, because I am scared." She wished she could be saying these things to Peter, her husband. The children helped because Mother Voran always worked side by side with them. She so longed for Peter, for his touch; she longed for him to call her Marta. No one seemed to call her Marta anymore.

The group of new immigrants had spent several months in the city in preparation for the move to the country and finally that move took place. Hanna felt a certain sadness and still she also sensed the atmosphere of anticipation. She would not return to the city again for a decade. Some 700 persons were moved hundreds of miles north into an area marked by a dense forest of tall, robust trees dotted with occasional clearings. The area had been chosen because it promised fertile soil, plenty of rain, and abundant timber.

Groups of families were taken to natural clearings in the forest. As the driver unloaded their meager belongings, he simply said, "Well, now you are at home." An ominous feeling came over the heads of households as everyone pondered what the future might hold, and, more immediately, how the first night might be spent. Children, on the other hand, only saw an adventuresome campout. Setting up camp was indeed the first task. The tents, which had been brought along, became home for the first few weeks. Families with male adults were much faster in building permanent quarters, but for the Voran family it was a major challenge. While the boys, now in their early teens, helped, it was still Mother who was the adult leader.

The next weeks were spent arranging essential living conditions. A stove-oven combination was built outside using mud from a nearby lagoon. An outhouse had to be built, plans had to be made for a house, and land needed to be prepared for farming. Everyone helped and worked from sunrise to sunset. Every fifth day, the community wagon and team of oxen became available to the family. On that day, two activities took place. First, some previously cut heavy timber was brought to the construction site until enough timber would be accumulated to build a house. It was an arduous task. The two-wheeled wagon was positioned right on center over the heavy timber, which was then hoisted up with a system of large pulleys and chains, and allowed to hang from the axle during transport. The oxen moved only if coaxed constantly with a long, pointed stick. Jagged, long scars testified of many years of unwilling work the animals had endured and the trickle of blood from the same scars spoke of the deep-seated resistance against an activity foreign to their constitution.

As time permitted, a few rows were also plowed for planting. Two people led the team of oxen, one held the plow, and two more people followed with the planting. Equipped with a bag holding the seeds, one person following the plow used the heel to stump a hole every ten or twelve inches into the freshly plowed soil, insert a seed or two, and the second person followed by covering the seed. Everyone helped.

Gradually, a routine was established. Evenings were passed sitting outside and talking, going to Wednesday evening Bible study, or to the village council meetings to plan community work. These meetings were for the heads of households with one vote per family. Men always represented the households, but widows were allowed to come—mostly to observe. Social norms did not permit them to participate in either the discussion or the vote, yet they were bound by the council decisions. As soon as a son in the household turned eighteen he was expected to represent the family, now given all rights and privileges of discussion and vote.

Life was miserably poor. The pioneers were totally dependent on nearby natural resources and their own ingenuity. In the absence of medical care, their bodies were mercilessly exposed to the ravages of tropical diseases. Death was forever a frequent visitor. Hanna remembered the little baby next door who died one afternoon. The funeral was to be the next day but there was no place to hold the body overnight. Wild animals attracted by the scent of death stalked the yard. The infant's father wrapped the tiny body in several blankets, then tied it to a rope and hung his lifeless bundle of love from a tree. All night long he stood guard, watching and protecting the now still clump of what had been life-of-his-life.

Eventually, the family was able to build a small home. Two large supporting hardwood trees with a strong Y branch at the top were dug into the ground at a distance of some twenty feet from each other. Another strong cross branch connected the two, inserting it into the Ys. This formed the centerline of the future house. Similar posts, but with lower Ys were placed at the four corners and connected to each other and with the roofline. Parallel branches running the length of the roof provided a solid support for the straw cover.

The roofing assembly line began in the mud hole where bundles of straw were dipped one end into the mud, thereby providing good binding material. These were then passed to a person standing next to the hole, who threw the bundle to the person sitting on the roofing slats. The catching had to be done somewhat artistically so as not to disintegrate the bundle in the process, nor end up with a mud-splattered face. Each bundle was then carefully placed so that the mud-drenched end lay flat on a slat for binding support. After weeks of making mud bricks, the sides were then slowly closed in, brick by heavy brick. Three boards nailed together with a cross slat served as the only door and empty commodity sacks became window covers.

It felt so good to be able to sit down in the evenings to rest and talk. Often, Hanna asked her mother to tell her about Russia. She usually complied by talking about the old estate, the house, which really was a mansion, the food, the cold winters, the neighbors, the skating, her horses, and so on. But tonight Hanna had a different request.

"Tell me about Daddy."

Mother was silent for a long time. In her mind, she retraced many experiences that had been hard, yet were rooted in a good feeling. Deep feelings of sadness welled up in her but she did want her children to know their past. The tropical night surrounded them with its typical multitude of sounds and smells. It provided a peaceful setting to relive the past. She began to relate.

"When I was a very young girl in Russia life was very good. We lived as we pleased and enjoyed our neighbors and ourselves. But life became difficult after the revolution and especially during the war. Everyone was looking for a place where we would be welcome, where we could worship in peace, farm the land, teach our children, and not serve in the army but do healing services instead. Many talked about moving to Canada. I think my dad wanted to move, too, but we had many relatives and it made it very difficult to leave them behind. So we decided not to leave.

"By 1930, things really got bad. Farmers had to give up most of their wheat for taxes. Some people simply abandoned their farms and went west. We heard rumors that most of these people died of starvation on the way.

"Government officials came to our village to organize collective farms. All of our tools, machines, and livestock had to be given to a common holding place. Men, women, and children were all expected to work in the fields. Older people worked in the vegetable gardens. We had so little to eat and my father bloated from starvation. As we worked, we talked and thought of nothing but food.

"But even in such difficult times there was joy. I met your father at our ice skating rink. He was tall, dark-haired, and very strong. We were married in 1934. My father was not very keen on the idea. For one thing, he thought this was much too young, but more than that the young lad I was seeing was not right; he did not belong to us, and he was too poor. Your dad and his mother had nothing and he wanted so much to have a home. We did get a marriage license and then rode the buggy some thirty miles to an old blind preacher who married us secretly. I don't remember what the preacher said, but I think he recited something from Proverbs. With us at the wedding party were only two others, the minister's wife and a servant. The next Sunday we had a little celebration at home—but no sermon. For lunch, we had borscht and to buy the bread my father had to walk ten miles. Once we got married, your dad was allowed to work on our collective farm.

"From 1937 to 1940, many men were taken from their families and put in jail on any little pretense. We now had four little children. Hanna, you were not yet born. On January 4, 1941, your dad came home and said to me that he was to report to the police station the next day. We both knew that this was the time we both had feared for so long. We did not have to pack, because we had prepared some

56

things long ago. It was so good that he could at least come home first, because many men were taken right from the fields or at night while sleeping and then the police would search the whole house looking for suspicious items such as letters from overseas. We spent so many fearful nights. And now our last night was here."

She stopped talking and looked at Hanna's beautiful and innocent face. She thought of that last night when she and her husband lay embraced in fear with sweat and tears drenching their bodies. They cried as they kissed their salty bodies. They knew that momentous event were about to tear at them and pull them apart. It was a painful yet such joyous night. Why did it have to be that the source of happiness also became the fountain for pain? She again looked at Hanna with her hair gleaming softly in the moonlight and wondered why it must be that the most beautiful gem is produced only under the most painful stress. Yes, the fairest of them all had been conceived, carried, and delivered under torments and tears. She indeed was a jewel.

"Yeah, that's when Hanna was conceived." She said it quietly to herself, forgetting for a moment that her children might still be awake.

"What did you say, Mother?"

"Oh, I was just thinking about the by-gone good old times." She hoped her children would not pursue their question.

Mother Voran was quiet for a long time as everyone pursued their own thoughts.

"Why don't you tell more, Mom?" Hanna's innocence broke the silence.

With the corner of her apron, Mother wiped a tear rolling down her cheek, and then continued.

"Well, the next day we both went to the station. It was such a difficult time, but we comforted ourselves with the thought that I was permitted to stay home, since often mothers were also taken.

"Your dad had often spoken of farewell and also mentioned that when our time came I should be strong and courageous, because then it would be easier for him. He had seen women scream and faint when they told their husbands good-bye. He did not want to remember me that way. He wanted to remember me as a strong wife.

I was able to control myself when we said good-bye for the last time. But later I cried a lot and often lost courage.

"The next day was my birthday. I was now twenty-seven. Your dad had given me my present several days before and asked me to open it on my birthday. That was also the day we moved in with your grandfather.

"I never learned what he was accused of. They told us that he was to be reeducated and that they would then send him back. But they never did. The police always acted as though he was guilty of some big crime. I was always hoping for a letter, but none came.

"Hanna, you were born on September 3. In the hospital, the other women had their husbands come to see them, and I lay there by myself.

"You remember your friend Katja? Her mom became very upset and was so afraid they would take her husband, too. She had to be taken to a mental institution for several weeks. She returned before she was well, and three days later they took her husband."

By now it had gotten darker. The half-moon hid behind the trees, and Hanna's brothers and sisters had gathered in a tight clump to listen intently as she continued.

"Katja's mother often came to us at night because she was afraid they would come and burn her house down. We often walked with her in the deep snow back to her house. She developed a severe knee infection and we took her to a hospital ten miles away. Your grandpa took her in the sled. She was in so much pain and often groaned all night long.

"We never heard from our husbands again. We sent many letters and sometimes even some money. I mentioned that you had been born and told him your name. I hope that if they did not give him the letters, maybe they at least told him your name. Once the police told me that your dad had been sentenced to ten years of labor in Siberia.

"After the war with Germany started, they took many of us to dig trenches. Mothers with young children did not have to go, but since I lived with your grandfather, they did call me, too. Hanna, you noticed something was going on and just clung to me day and night before I went. I had promised you that if I had to go at night I would first wake you. Well, they came at night and I woke you up. They took us by train across the river where we had to dig trenches, deep and wide, and endlessly long. We hadn't worked very long when we heard the bombs from the German front. When an airplane came, we ran across the fields to hide.

"Once the trench was too deep and I could not get out on time so I just pressed against the wall but was not hurt by the falling bombs. The Germans got closer and closer but we had to keep on digging, and one evening the order to evacuate did come. But because the Germans had overrun us, we could not return. We, as Germans, were prisoners of the Germans. Suddenly, they set us free. We found some horses and headed back. We met a man who told us that our villages had been destroyed and that all the people had left. My heart sank. Everybody was depressed. One man in our group said that if he did not find his family at home he would commit suicide.

"Ten miles before getting to our village, someone told us that the Russians had not deported our village since the railroad tracks were destroyed. What an indescribable, joyous reunion we had. But you, Hanna, did not recognize me and there was no letter from your dad either. I hurt immensely!"

Mother asked if they wanted to go to bed, but tonight they were wide awake and wanted to hear more.

"It wasn't long before the Russians forced the German army back and we, too, had to flee. We packed a few things on the wagon and let Grandpa ride while the rest of us walked. We had only been going one day when it began to rain and the mud made it very hard to continue. We took some things off the wagon, set them by the road, and went on. For a while, we stayed in abandoned houses but as the war came closer, we had to keep going. The road got worse, the horses were hungry and tired, their hoofs started bleeding, and it became more difficult finding somewhere to stay. We had lice all over us. Your grandpa was not feeling well and just wanted to die along the road. Soon, some wagons joined us and we repacked our loads. Grandpa went on with others and I was left with you children. I was so scared.

"We had to travel up steep inclines always with one side of the wagon close to the ravine. It was here where the wagon broke. We had to stay and find help to get it fixed while the others in our group

59

went on. Fortunately, the people where we stopped were very helpful. They even put us up in nice beds. I did not want to sleep in those beds because we were dirty and had lice, but they insisted. We met many nice Russians.

"For five weeks we traveled by wagon when it began to snow. Often I stayed nights in the wagon by myself while some kind strangers took you children in for the night. One day, I heard that Grandpa had died. Grandpa had found lodging with a Russian family who really did not want to have them because they had a wedding. He was on his deathbed while the wedding party got drunk. They said in his last days he constantly kept calling for me. Later, I found out he had died only three miles from where we were. I visited his grave.

"One time the front caught up with us. The Russian soldiers exchanged our horses for old and weak ones. They also took things from our wagon. Later, they even took the old horses. We had to pack a few things onto a sled and pull it as we fled.

"Along the road we got stopped many times for documents or they wanted our coats or shoes, or what little we had left. One day a soldier stopped, looked at me, and hit me across the face so hard that I fell into the ditch. My face was swollen for many days.

"In the spring, after the snow started to melt, they made us dig a huge grave for all the corpses along the road. Once I dug up a soldier's arm and to this day, I cannot forget the shock. Sometimes we found addresses on the soldiers. I felt so sorry for the mothers or wives who must be at home waiting for some news.

"Just before we reached the train to take us across the border into Germany we saw Katja with her brothers and sisters. They had gotten lost since their mother was always sick and the children had to find their own way. She had died on the wagon and the children had continued walking for 24 hours with the body of their mother in the wagon. Finally, someone had offered to bury her and then given them directions to meet us.

"I miss Peter—your father."

It was late and Hanna had fallen asleep with her head propped onto her mother's lap. Mother took her children to bed so that all could rest for the next day's calling of hard work, work, work.

4

Ernesto first saw her during the Thursday youth evening. At first sight, he was mesmerized and stunned frozen solid to the ground; a thread of icy sweat ran down his back. Her flowing white dress gave radiance to her person. While in the company of other girls, she seemed to take center stage—not because she demanded it or even wanted it, but because of the special vitality and glow she brought with her. The room she entered seemed to come alive with her bright laughter, her sparkling eyes. Her movements were quick yet purposeful, strong and determined, yet ever so graceful. Her laughter carried a hint of childish giggle, but its honest spontaneity and gaiety showed a lust for life contagious to those around her. Her laughter, her words, and her body language all evolved naturally from her inner self. She overflowed with self-confidence based on her knowledge that life is good and happy.

She had just arrived from the rugged country where she had finished all available schooling by age sixteen. She had liked school. Her quick wit, lively mind, and exploratory spirit were the right ingredients for a positive experience. She particularly enjoyed physical education activities. Having been blessed with a coordinated body and quick muscles she was able to outdo everyone, including the boys.

Her body developed early and did so in a most exquisite manner. By age twelve she had blossomed, looking like a fresh bud about to open. A strange new sensation came over her as she entered her flowering adolescence and she noticed her evolving body and the sudden attention from boys, both her age and older. The attention came in the form of competition to be in her presence, competition on the athletic field, where they ran desperately so as to remain close to her, or the frequent male companionship she enjoyed on the walks home from school. She sensed the ownership of something wildly feminine about her. It pleased her and gave her confidence.

Her two older sisters had left home soon after age sixteen to work as maids in the city. The small farming community did not provide many opportunities for girls, and so it was that in 1958, when she turned seventeen, she, too, departed for the city. Her mother's departing words "Work hard and you can't fail. If you do a good job people will notice and you will be given opportunities, and you'll keep alive," had a familiar ring by now. In the city, her life would be changed forever.

At seventeen, Hanna had reached the full bloom of womanhood in a body beaming with firm youth. Her upright shoulders framed an erect torso, which yielded down to a narrow waist. Of average stature, she was extremely well coordinated; all her movements were a pleasing sight. Too new in the city to be stifled by social barriers, she moved through the world with the same innocent assurance she had felt in the wilds of her forest home. She seemed to be charged with electricity and one could almost sense the powerful radiation of her femininity. The white dress, so utterly becoming, highlighted her tan and matched her hair.

Her blond, shoulder-length hair was kept in smooth, flowing waves. Parted on the left, the falling waves seemed to provide the perfect frame for her face. Her face was oval, her complexion flawless, and her nostrils teaming and eagerly inhaling the air of life. When she spoke and smiled her fresh, full lips parted engagingly from the center out. The left side of her lower lip displayed a most unusual dimple, which became more pronounced as she smiled. It made her even more arrestingly attractive. However, most fascinating were those big blue eyes. Perfectly matching the contrasting natural red of the lips and marble white of her skin, her sapphire-blue eyes seemed to shine with expectation of things to come.

Ernesto was taken with the absolute symmetry of her features and purity of life. He could not help but feed his eyes on the wonder of it all. This gift from heaven was wrapped in a body that glorified perfect womanhood; it celebrated rich strength harvested from the wilderness she had just left.

At nineteen, Ernesto had been coming to these Thursday evening community youth gatherings for nearly two years. The evenings provided a proper setting for relaxation, sports, games, and, most of all, interaction and matchmaking. Ernesto had enjoyed these evenings with his friends and had watched with excitement, yet some despair, how his friends, one by one, had found their female counterparts and were now off to better things. But it did not seem to matter much, especially since his friends were generally a few years older and were more developed. He looked at his body and saw a tall, scrawny kid with yet no real need to shave, with legs too long for the torso, pants that seemed never able to keep pace with the growing body, and hair that would not stay in place unless forced with dried-on soap. Thus far, he had had no girlfriend. Sure, there had been interest—mostly on his part—and even an occasional date, but no permanent relationship. He did show some interest in local Spanish girls from school, however, that seemed to be frowned upon by the immigrant community in this city of the tropics, and his parents as well. Nevertheless, Estella Sisa, a general's daughter, often kept his mind occupied and his imagination going wild. After school, he walked home behind her pretending to be her friend telling himself that if no girl from his people crossed his life, then Estella certainly would be very nice.

His friend Herman had coaxed him repeatedly to pay attention to his sister. Elsie was nice, very eager, and available. The chemistry was never right, in part, since no conquest was involved.

Instead, Ernesto enjoyed sitting with his friends in Bar San Roque sipping *café con leche.* The restaurant, a landmark in the ancient city of the *conquistadores,* had seen better days when nobles entered its doors to see and be seen. It had been the hub of the aristocracy where upper society rumors were spun and transmitted, where budding politicians, who loved to hear themselves speak, practiced their trade on an uninterested audience. Today, only the yard-thick walls and high ceilings spoke of its glorious past. Today, the shoeshine boys were free to crawl under the tables pushing on clients' shoes to get the attention of potential costumers. Still, the *café con leche* seemed not to have lost its fame. Ernesto and his friends liked the lingering pretend atmosphere. Here they could feel superior by ordering from the eagerly submissive white-uniformed waiters and commanding the shoeshine boys about.

On Saturday mornings, he and his friends joined the city in the age-old ritual of girl-watching. Traffic on Main Street was blocked off ostensibly for the shoppers' convenience. Pedestrians, old and young alike, freely roamed about the street to search, watch, admire, give the familiar two-tone whistle of approval to a deserving girl parading past, and allow the heart to pretend and imagine.

Yes, he was well aware that his parents had moved the family to the city some years ago for the sole purpose of providing better educational opportunities—a highly prized commodity with the immigrants. The early settlement years had kept everyone at essentially the same financial level, but a cast system developed with the religious and educational leaders at the top. Ernesto was a child of that leadership and hence expectations on him were high. He spent his time at studies, which, fortunately, he enjoyed immensely. He spent hours reading the Spanish classics. Juan Valera's *Pepita Jiménez* brought boundless joy, giving him first exposure to what true love is. He extended his intellectual horizon by taking private lessons in typing, correspondence courses in electronics, and he spent much time in self-development in the arts, literature, and science, detailing his own inventions, making intricate drawings, ordering parts, and assembling scientific devices. He reaped endless hours of enjoyment from building a radio from scratch. A part-time job provided the needed cash to support his noble ambitions. It was a happy time of development.

Yet, it was on Thursday evenings, when the excitement of gathered youth surrounded him, that he began to feel an emptiness, a longing, a searching for something he could not describe. He did sense that its fulfillment, when it came, would bring something utterly new and beautiful.

That following Thursday evening a volleyball game was in full swing when he arrived. His eyes immediately fell on the girl, again dressed in pure white, who ever so gracefully maneuvered the ball from every possible and seemingly impossible angle. Her mocking laughter showed a fascinating self-assurance. Someone called her "Hanna." He let his imagination wander, pretending to be talking with her, offering to take her home (the proper first approach in showing an interest), or even taking her to the movies. As he pondered these visions, the game concluded and he suddenly saw her coming toward him, walking past him, and smiling gaily. The rest of the evening he felt stiff and uncoordinated as he tried to muster the needed courage to talk to someone with so much zest for life, someone apparently so special. He could not bring himself to look at her, let alone speak to her, and eventually she left in the company of other girls. He watched her disappear into the night, a night during which he lay awake a long time.

All that week his thoughts returned to that girl in white. He was not really interested in school activities, his self-studies now became daydreaming sessions, and his part-time job was only perfunctory. He was waiting for Thursday, and when the next Thursday finally came, she was not there. All evening he went through the motions of being part of the youth group but was constantly looking. He did not want to ask anyone about her for fear of his intent being found out. He did not even know her last name. On Sunday, he did see her profile during church services. Since he was sitting to the side and several rows behind her, he was free to steal glances without being found out. The formal atmosphere, however, did not allow for communication and so he had to be content to look occasionally and wait for next Thursday. This time she was there.

A game had been planned with all the youth sitting in a large circle, and singing songs. During the beginning of each song a boy went up to a girl and bowed slightly, whereupon she hopefully rose, took his arm, and they walked in the circle while singing along. Ernesto did participate by choosing other girls during the first two times. He did not want his interest to seem too obvious. However, throughout the process he watched her. Obviously, she was being invited every time. How could one help but be attracted to such a radiant beauty? He thought that he had noticed her glance just at the beginning of the second song, but did not find the courage either to return the glance or to ask her.

But then, as though carried by an impulse given only to those determined to shape their destiny, he did walk up to her at the onset of the third song. She smiled, her hand slipped gently into his arm, and he walked as if in a daze. She walked with a hint of haughtiness, her head held high. Something began to tremble deep inside him. It was that magic moment during which a boy was being transformed into a new being—a man. At the end of the song he escorted her to her seat and heard himself asking, "May I take you home tonight?" She did not answer but only smiled. He thought that perhaps the singing had been too loud and that she had not heard him. He was flowing in uncertainty and took as his consolation that maybe, just maybe, she really had not heard him, or that she was shy. He did not ask again just then, but decided to take a chance later.

After the evening wore down, he did notice that she lingered about and he immediately took that as a signal, walked up to her, and asked again: "May I take you home?" Her "Okay" would change his life forever.

They walked stiffly side by side to the station where the electric trolley #10 departed. Her name was Hanna Voran, she had arrived from the country just a few weeks ago, and she worked as a maid for people who lived on Avenida Santísimo Sacramento. As they approached the station, he recognized the gong signaling the imminent trolley arrival and departure and asked, "Do you want to run to catch it?" As though struck by lightening she bolted for the trolley. Ernesto, who with his long legs had generally been able to hold his own in most circumstances, found himself trailing the girl in the white dress. They caught the trolley, he paid the fare, and they found two seats. Panting breathlessly, they looked at each other and smiled. He was in awe of her delightful wild carelessness displayed so simply. The conversation and close proximity gave him proper excuses to look at her face. He saw such dazzling loveliness and wondered how it might be that other fellows had not snapped her up before him. What he felt was so new, so enchanting. His head seemed to be swimming with joy.

The home she worked in on Avenida Santísimo Sacramento was some ten blocks from the trolley station. Being removed from the center of the city, the street was dark and untraveled. The houses on either side were dimly lit and hidden behind the profuse vegetation of the tropics. Loud radio music seemed to hammer from a home providing the evening entertainment interrupted only occasionally by a barking dog. As they approached the last block, the street inclined as evidenced by the rain-scarred terrain.

The home of her masters was separated from the street by a low, white-washed brick fence and a row of tall eucalyptus trees that seemed to be the preferred home of noisy summer bugs. They talked a bit and then she reached for the door. He quickly asked, "Are you going to be there next Thursday?" She nodded and went inside.

It was a long but happy ride home. He had been struck by lightening: his longing for her. He felt as in a bottomless depth of bliss with his soul soaring higher and the feelings running deeper. Could this be love, first love? From that day on an intense passion would ignite within him—but so would eventual deep suffering.

5

The next Thursday he managed again to be at the right place at the right time and thus have the privilege to take her home. He knew that the more often he could do this, the likelier his chances of eventually claiming her as his prize. The cycle repeated itself on several succeeding Thursdays. Each encounter was an opportunity to be just a little bit closer to her, to speak just a bit more daringly, to ask more probing questions. Eventually he knew that he wanted to reach the place where he could ask her out to occasions other than just taking her home from the predictably programmed Thursday evening youth gatherings. That was the goal.

And his overtures were met with positive signals. She smiled willingly, allowed his closer approach, and gleefully answered his questions. She even began to ask questions about him and his life. In fact, he thought he noticed an air of anticipation on her part: expectation that he would come to take her home on Thursday evenings. Once when she was still busily talking to her friends after the youth gathering she glanced over to where he was. He appeared to be ready to go—at least he was at that moment not talking with anyone. He noticed that she quickly broke off her conversation with her friends in order to be ready to go—so it appeared to him. And indeed, they then left together. Ernesto felt he had reached a point in his relationship with her where both expected and enjoyed each other's company. But then came the blow.

The youth group had planned a trip to a city park for fun and games. It was a large park with huge eucalyptus trees, fountains, flower beds, bird sanctuaries, and wide roads winding through the greens. As with most public places it also was named after one of the historical heroes of the perceived glorious past of the country. Parque Caballero overlooked the wide bay, which a few miles away held the city harbor. City lights reflected in the waters and the slowly moving ships seemed like swans gliding on still waters. The peaceful beauty was deceiving though. The park's boundary toward the water ended abruptly as the ground fell steeply some hundred feet toward the water.

Between the abyss and the waters lay a strip of land densely occupied by squatters. Two thirds of the city's population lived in these shanties at the edge of the water where people relieved themselves in the open air. The excrement dried in the sun, turned to dust, and became part of the air everyone inhaled. The stench and filth of the slums was cleared only during the occasional flooding when all straw huts were washed away and the dwellers were forced to evacuate until the waters subsided.

Tonight though, it seemed that the odor from below the park's edge was drifting in the opposite direction. The youth group had picked a clearing and was engaged in a series of games, one of which involved the picking of a member to be blindfolded.

Ernesto and Hanna had come separately to the outing as part of the larger group. They saw each other, but somehow were not together. Ernesto marveled at the fluidity with which she seemed to move through the crowd, but he also noticed the attention she was receiving from the male population. She was as happy as ever, seeming to laugh at her own laughter. Eli in particular seemed to stick very close to her. He would be an obvious competitor—clever, quick witted, silver-tongued, well built, dark complexion, and well matured for his age, with a business mind that had been widely recognized. His ingenuity in arranging human affairs had brought him several substantial business deals that were the envy of all. Most recently, he received the contract to demolish an old building. It was unheard of for such a young man. Eli, of course, reveled in his success.

Ernesto was not sure if Eli's overture was an intrusion into what he had considered his domain, whether Eli just did not know, or whether this was simply a test to check the seriousness of the young relationship. When it was Ernesto's turn to be blindfolded, he did so with trepidation and his fears were confirmed. When he was freed of his blindfold neither Hanna nor Eli was to be found anywhere. He could feel his blood rushing violently through his body. His ears were aflame, as he experienced for the first time the jealousy of the unfair kingdom of love. Perhaps he had assumed too much. Of course, he had never mentioned anything to Hanna about how much he cared for her. He thought perhaps she would have known through the attention he had given her that she indeed was very special to him. Perhaps he

69

now needed to make stronger overtures; else, he was going to lose her.

Ernesto sensed his whole being rushing toward her. He could not fathom life without her. To his happy surprise, he did find her quite happy to be taken home again the following Thursday evening as though nothing had happened. He justified this carefree action of hers as just that: she still felt, and obviously was, quite free. From now on, when taking her home he would watch for every possible opportunity to make proper physical contact with her such as holding her arm as she entered the tram, or brushing against her while walking. A fire had ignited in his veins and was burning throughout his body. This fire was fueled by the need for conquest. To his delight, he soon noticed that the alert youth group soon stamped the match accomplished and Hanna no longer responded to other male attention.

During a volleyball game Ernesto missed a spike and someone from the other court called, "Come on, Voran!" He did not know what to make of it. Was it someone's jealousy? Was it someone's way of announcing a new pair? Was it mocking, cynicism? It hurt, but it also was pride.

Not only did he again take her home, but he resolved to make arrangement to also meet and take her home Sunday after church—a first non-Thursday risk.

"Are you going to be in church on Sunday?" he asked, knowing full and well that she always did come, but he wanted to direct her attention toward that new possibility.

"Yes, I am planning to be there."

"Can I meet you after church?"

"Okay."

It felt good that she accepted, because it indeed did indicate clearly that the relationship had gone a step beyond that of the chance encounter. They smiled as they parted.

"I'll see you in the morning," he said playfully.

"Sunday is still a few days away," she reminded him.

"Okay."

6

They were sitting on the low, white-washed wall in front of the home on Avenida Santísimo Sacramento. The summer bugs chirped loudly proclaiming the benefits of tropical summer heat. It was Sunday evening—not Thursday. Ernesto was flushed with pride and happiness of the accomplished conquest. She had allowed him to take her home after Sunday evening church services. The new stage in their relationship not only gave a sense of security but also familiarity.

"Tell me about you," he said.

"What do you want to know?"

"Anything, as long as it is about you. Why don't you start with when you left Russia?"

Her thoughts went back to Russia a long time ago, when her mother had been gone to some far off place to work. She and her brothers and sisters had to go live with Grandfather. They had always liked to go there, but it was not the same to be there without Mom. Besides, they had to help with the chores. When they used to go for Christmas or Easter they could just play and play.

Grandpa was talking about the war and about moving away. Sometimes in the night, she remembered hearing shooting in the distance. It made her wonder about her mother and she was afraid.

"Well, are you going to tell me about your trip from Russia?" Ernesto wondered.

Hanna nodded, staring down at her hands. Then she continued.

"One night, my mother came back from a far away place where she'd had to work and everybody was in a hurry to pack. The grown-ups had decided to leave and move to another country. I remember being told that I could only take a few things along. One thing I did pack was the doll Katja and I used to play house with. Katja and her mom were leaving, too, but I was not supposed to tell anybody that we were leaving."

"Who was Katja?" Ernesto asked.

"She was my best friend and lived next door. Her father, too, had been banned to Siberia.

"One night, we started out with the wagons. Grandpa and I were loaded on the wagon and the others walked. Katja and her family were on another wagon. I remember I could not sleep well and that it rained. It was kind of cold. Some of the men went out into the city to buy things. Mom said that no one could take any money out of the country, so they were spending it. Grandpa was no longer with us.

"When we got onto the train everybody was happy, but I did not like it because I had no room. Everybody was crowded with all their things and there were not enough seats. Lots of people were sick and coughed all night. I remember how quiet it always got when the men in uniform with their red-rimmed caps came through. Everybody looked scared. The uniformed men looked at some papers and then left. They came every day, sometimes several times whenever the train stopped.

Ernesto was not sure if he wanted to hear more, but then, he had asked her to relate stories of Russia. He decided not to interfere, but to endure.

"I remember the fearful incident one day when the train stopped and some people in the wagon in front of ours got out. They started digging in the dirt, but it was hard. I recognized some of the men from our village. Then they brought a lady out who had a bundle in her arms and she cried loudly. Mom said that her baby had died during the night. They said a prayer, took the baby, and laid it in the hole. The hole was not very deep; I could still see the baby. So they had to get some loose dirt to cover it up. The mother cried louder and louder and knelt down by the grave. She tried to push the dirt back and get the baby. But they held her back. Then the mother started running away from the train toward the forest. Some people had to run to go get her. She kept on crying and saying, 'They took my husband. I don't want to leave my baby here, no, no, don't leave my baby here, I want to stay, too. I'm not going along, I want to stay.' I could hear her cry for a long time.

"The next day, my mother and I went to the next wagon to see the mother whose baby had died. I remember how she sat there in a corner without expression on her face. But what I remember most is that the lady's hair had, over night, turned completely gray. Mother said she was only twenty-eight years old."

The sound of the noisy summer bugs overhead seemed out of place, but Ernesto did not notice. He was allowed a glimpse into the life he cared about. They sat silently, and then Hanna continued.

"One afternoon, everybody was excited because the train crossed a red gate. They said that this was the end of Russia. People were happy and cried and sang church songs.

"I remember how nice it was when we got to the shelter. The people there were good to us. They spoke German, they had white coats on, they smiled, and they checked everybody's eyes and gave everybody enough to eat. I liked that, and I liked that I could run all around the building and even to the orchard. There were lots of trees and grass and flowers. What I did not like was that everybody had to sleep in that same big building. Each family just had some blankets that they hung around to mark off some rooms. No one was supposed to be noisy. Sometimes the men had meetings. Mom told us that they were making plans to move to a far away country."

Hanna thought of the two ships that had brought them from Europe to this new home. The big ocean liner had a most magnificent impact on all. It was so huge and so graceful. Its white-uniformed stewards, its deep sounding horn, its many decks, the food, and the possibilities for endless explorations had made the ship a fun home for many weeks. It was loaded with thousands of people all going to South America.

She did not really care that the ship was apparently operated by an inept crew and had been launched without proper inspection and outfitting. Both the rudder and the engines gave out and the ship floated aimlessly for weeks. Instead of the normal three weeks, it took seven weeks to cross the ocean.

She did remember some unpleasant times, like the crowds of people pushing on the decks when there was something to see, or the bad food, or when she got sea sick. But mostly she had fond memories of that big floating home. The people were nice, the ocean was so blue, the weather pleasant, and getting warmer, and food and drink were plentiful—a new experience for her. Their family all lived in one cabin and it had a big fan on the ceiling. She thought that was interesting.

She remembered docking at some islands one day. What impressed her most were all the vendors along the dock selling their goods. Besides toys, and clothing, she saw many, many oranges, other strange looking fruit, and large straw hats. Everybody seemed to speak a different language. She wondered if she would have to learn such a strange language.

In the evenings, the people would gather on the deck to sing, have a church service, or a meeting to plan how they were going to live once they got to their destination. She was interested in all of this and often sat on the floor and listened. During one such meeting, the men and widows all drew straws to see which village they would move to and in what order they would settle in each village. She had memorized all the names of the families that were supposed to live with them in the same village.

After some silence Ernesto said, "I am still listening."

"We sailed across the Atlantic in 1948 on the *Charlton Monarch* and after many weeks of towing by another ship we could see the coast of South America far off in the distance and then the city of Rio de Janeiro revealed itself slowly on the horizon. As the ship drew nearer, the blue ocean waters became brown and murky. Slowly the ship appeared to be engulfed by an ocean not of water, but of city buildings. On the dock, life was busy with trucks coming and going, tall cranes lifting boxes out of ships, and cars and people dashing about.

"Eventually, we sailed down to the La Plata and soon we noticed a smaller ship slowly approaching ours and then attaching itself like a chick to the mother duck. It was the river boat *Ciudad de Buenos Aires,* which was to take us up the river to our destination. For the next several hours, people said good-bye to all the friends they had made among the stewards, maids, and cooks, and then moved their belongings to the smaller boat.

"It was evening when we sat down in the small dining room in the new ship for bean soup when the *Ciudad de Buenos Aires* departed on its three-day trip north. The next day I had a chance to explore the new floating home. With only three decks, it was not difficult at all. What surprised me was the lower deck where people traveled third class. They were all in one big open room with their things on the floor next to them. Many people had strung hammocks between posts and slept in shifts. Some people even made little coal fires right on the ship floor and cooked their food. They all seemed content. In the evening, there was a lot of music coming from the lower deck. Several men would get together and play guitars and sing. One evening, a man with a harp joined them. They played very nicely. During the day, and even at night, many people would fish and talk to pass the time.

"We lived in the middle deck. All the rest of the immigrants seemed to have a good time. Everybody was excited about seeing their new homeland. The young people even had choir practice.

"The food was awful—beans, rice, and lots of meat. The bread was very new. It actually was really not bread but a very hard roll the waiters called *galletas*. I liked them but many people could not bite into them. And there were so many new fruits I had never seen or tasted before. Besides oranges, there were grapefruit, bananas, papayas, pineapples, and pomegranates.

"I remember the waiters using their towels to wipe the sweat off their face, and then use the same towel to clean the table and dry the dishes. They got water by dipping a bucket into the river at the back of the ship, and I knew that the bathrooms were at the front.

"We liked to sit on the front deck and watch the countryside. We could hear the splashing sound the water made as the hull sliced through the waves. I liked that sound. Sometimes other boats would pass or little canoes would come up close and a passenger would get on or off. There were also many water plants that came floating down the river. They had huge leaves and sometimes a big red flower in the center.

"Once we saw the bony head of a dead cow floating in the water. My brothers told me that the river was full of vicious *piraña* fish, which attack and devour anything that moves in the water. That was the first time I heard about the fish that have extremely sharp teeth and their jaws move back and forth when they bite. They said that when a farmer wants to drive a herd of cattle through the river he is afraid that the *piraña* fish will eat them all. So, he sends in an old cow first. It is eaten by the fish as it floats downstream, and then the rest of the herd can safely enter the water."

Hanna remembered off on the shore the many things new to her. Big trees were everywhere, but the palm trees were most interesting with their straight stems, a crown of leaves, and bundles of coconuts. Once she saw a monkey eating coconuts at the top of a palm tree. There were many different colors of flowers everywhere she looked. Some people lived along the shore in little mud huts. She thought of the Garden of Eden where Adam and Eve lived among all the colorful plants and animals.

Some places she saw strange carts with two huge wheels being pulled very slowly by two oxen; it had been her first introduction to the *carreta*. A man in the cart had a long stick with which he prodded the oxen to go faster.

One day she even saw Indians on the dock of a little town where the ship stopped. They had such colorful bird feathers all around their brown bodies. They sold bows, arrows, and animal skins.

Ernesto sat enjoying the sound of Hanna's voice. He was glad destiny had brought her close, that they lived at the same time at the same place, and that she affected him as she did. The summer bugs still chirped away, but off in the distance the big cathedral bell Maria Angola struck ten o'clock. It was a familiar sound of peace.

7

"People are known by the company they keep. So, son, be careful whom you associate yourself with." Ernesto and his father walked to church as the lesson in poorly disguised clothing came.

"You remember Mr. Reimer?" his father continued. "He started out real good in life, but then became ensnarled with the wrong kind of people. His luck ran out on him, he lost his job, and look what he is doing now. You remember him, don't you?"

"Yes, I do, Dad." He had heard the story many times.

"I remember a friend I had when I was young. He got involved with the wrong kind of woman; she was just not of his type and..."

Ernesto knew the conversation was going to turn this direction. He suspected that his father knew about Hanna and this was his way of letting him know what he thought about the matter. While Dad continued talking, Ernesto kept quiet, listened, but did not hear. How could Dad make a judgment without ever having taken the time to talk with her? Was he implying she was the "wrong kind of woman?" Ernesto could not wait to get to the church when he could go his own way and not be reminded of the old, uncomfortable lessons. Once he got to church he would choose a seat toward the back so he could look over to the women's side and, with luck, she would sit someplace where he could see her.

"The only road to success is education." The fatherly advice repeated itself in familiar fashion. "You see, if you have an education it is something no one can take from you. But it does not come easily; it is won the hard way through many solitary hours of study, study, study. But you will never be sorry of the sacrifice you are making now. It will give you rewards beyond expectation. So, spend your time wisely—with books and the right kind of people."

Ernesto was glad when they entered the church door.

They had agreed they'd do the daring thing: meet Thursday at the usual youth event, but not stay and instead go to the movies. It was a slow walk through town that just a few hours before had been drenched by a torrential rain. The streets, which served as the city's only storm sewer, were still carrying rivers of filth-laden water. The saving rains thus not only watered life, but cleansed life's byproducts as well. And the rains did come frequently enough that it was quite natural to dispose refuse into the streets where either stray dogs or the rain would clear it away.

There was now more comfort between Hanna and Ernesto then there had been just a short while back. Both loved the familiar sights, sounds, and even smells of the city as they negotiated the city's waterways. Native music seemed to be coming from so many directions. The typical harp and the ever present guitar penetrated the early evening air. Down a ways, the loud clanging sound of a passing trolley car made its periodic gong sounds at each intersection. These museum-like antiquities had been a part of the city since 1907 and continued to claim their place as landmarks in daily life. A paperboy crying in a high-pitched voice *Tribuna, Tribuna, Tribuna...* attempted to sell the last of his papers. Here and there sat a tight circle of men in undershirts sipping *tereré* tea from the communal gourd and metal straw. Life was peaceful on the way downtown.

As they crossed Antequera Street, they looked south and saw, a block away, the steeply rising street, which had no cobblestone but steps instead. The steps ascended for an entire city block until reaching the top where they culminated into a platform whose center held a huge column topped by the familiar statue of an angel. The Angel monument was whitewashed, surrounded by an ornate fence, and always busy with visitors strolling about leisurely.

"I remember that!" she exclaimed to her own surprise.

"When did you see it?" he inquired.

"Oh, about ten years ago, when we lived in town for several months. As kids we used to go downtown and I could always see that monument. But I never did get close to it and always wished I could."

Ernesto thought about changing plans and just spending the evening at The Angel, but chose to postpone such a visit.

Victoria Theater was a familiar setting. He had often gone to see movies—mostly by himself or with his friends. Recently, the touching love story in the *Titanic* had made a great impact on him as the young sailor expressed his ecstasy of love for his girl by flinging his cap into the far ocean waves. Her kiss rewarded him for his sacrifice, though she later lost him to the stillness of the deep below the waves. Here Ernesto and Hanna were to see many movies but tonight's performance was *Samson and Dilalah*.

"*Dos entradas, por favor.*"

"*Primera o segunda clase?*" the clerk asked.

"*Primera.*" Ernesto was pleased to buy first class tickets. As they entered the theater, Ernesto felt something new. Heads turned towards them. And well they should as the men noticed the stunning blond beauty by his side. In fact, the familiar two-tone whistle of appreciation could be heard. It was an uplifting feeling to receive such honest approval.

Entering the darkened room it felt proper to hold Hanna's arm and as they sat down he just continued the contact by sliding his hand down her arm to catch her hand. His fingers wove into hers and her forearm just fit inside his. She did not refuse this new overture and it was as though a curtain of doubt lifted from his mind. Throughout the movie, they held hands. At times the hard armrest between them became uncomfortable, but he did not readjust position for fear of losing the touch of her hand.

Hand in hand, they strolled through the adjoining park after the movies. The Pantheon of the Heroes monument stood proudly in the midst of the park landscape proclaiming a past more heroic in retrospect than in reality. Walking past the perpetual honor guards, they looked to quench their thirst stimulated by the long movie and the walk through the gardens. They found refreshment at Lido Bar, a place whose only resemblance to its original counterpart in Paris was the name. Nonetheless, the freshly made, cold pineapple juice was the best in town.

Because it was late, and to show his gentlemanliness, rather than taking the trolley car he hired a cab to take them to Avenida Santísimo Sacramento. There they sat outside on the low fence running along the street and talked for a long time. Their conversation was simple, but as full of meaning as the words of Solomon. Hanna enjoyed his voice, his tall, lean frame, and the intense brown eyes, which at this stage in life only could hint at the delayed bloom, which was eventually to launch him into a whirlwind of success. He put his right arm around her while holding left hands.

He reveled in the bliss of watching her sweet face drenched in the moonlight. Just enough light streamed through the tall eucalyptus trees to produce sparkles in her eyes. No eyes had ever awakened such joyous, dulcified emotion in his heart.

They sat quietly, allowing the moment's beauty to soak in. Then he pulled her shoulder close to his and kissed her cheek. The bold move seemed to turn his lips to wood, yet they quivered from the terror of love as he kissed her cheeks again and again. He explored the warmth of the hollow of her neck as he thought of her lips and wondered what a kiss on her mouth would be like.

He ran his index finger across the length of her lips and watched in astonishment as they bounced back into position with firm, healthy fullness. Then slowly, ever so slowly he lowered his mouth to hers, claiming her lips and finding warm, wet readiness. It seemed that the kiss was made in heaven. Both were aware of the shaking lips at this new experience, but as her arms slowly embraced his broad shoulders, then his neck, a confident calmness overcame them both. Playfully, her fingers ran through the hair in the back of his head giving a clear signal that the feelings were mutual. The evening wore on as they pursued the newly discovered passion of first love. It was not driven by sexual desire, but the simple need to experience the completeness that comes when two lives fuse into one, and which no one single human being can experience. Though they were two persons, they indeed were like a unified one. Two hearts alone in the shadows of the tall eucalyptus trees were beating in time to the rhythm of the harp music coming from somewhere across the hill. Their expression of love was so carefree, so spontaneous, and so natural. It was love giving itself for the first time. One soul in two bodies.

"I'll see you in the morning?" he asked jokingly, as he prepared to leave.

"Sure, since I have nothing to do tomorrow," she teased, as she went inside.

After falling in love, all things seemed to go better. Ernesto worked faster, longer, harder, and better. There no longer seemed any routine in life. All was new and rejuvenated. He felt himself arriving at a destination toward which he must have traveled all his life—and had he not found it, he would have never known that he was but a mere approximation of a man. Dear Lord, how beautiful and great the felicity!

It was Herman who first destroyed the bliss and put it most bluntly.

"What kind of girl is that anyhow whom you are dating? Didn't she just arrive from the country? What does she know about city life or about you? Is she going to go to school, or does she already know everything? In fact, what do you know about her?"

Ernesto was petrified, speechless with surprise and rage. Didn't Herman see the obvious? She was a dazzling beauty, an exuberant human spirit, one who had just changed his life and feeling about himself. And now his friend seemed to imply non-acceptability? Was this the Herman he had known since childhood? The same Herman with whom he had talked long hours in their earlier youth about their plans, and hopes, and about girls? He had always sought out Herman because he was fun to be with, always seemed to have an edge on life's experiences, and always had the newest desirable things. Just a few weeks ago, they, along with half a dozen other boys, had strolled daringly through the city on New Year's Eve. They had blocked traffic by walking eight abreast, arms locked across each other's shoulders and rhythmically goose-stepping sideways across each other's legs. He had been right next to Herman and enjoyed it immensely. But now he felt let down, misunderstood, by his friend.

"What are you guys going to do? Become farmers, ehh?" he continued relentlessly.

Ernesto's throat seemed to swell shut with a growing lump. He sought a quick parting and attempted to unravel the meaning of all this.

It was true no one had yet said a congratulatory word about the new union, he thought, but that certainly was due to the newness of the affair or the shyness of the observers. Certainly, in their hearts, everyone saw an arrangement made in heaven.

These same thoughts circled in his mind into the late evening.

8

The bicycle had never been so clean. As he was wiping each individual spoke in the front wheel, he suddenly whirled around in response to that familiar stern voice behind him.

"Where are you going?" his father asked.

Father had seen him come and go many times and rarely did inquire. Ernesto felt as though before an inquisition and his body language mirrored the inner fear.

"Just going for a ride." It was a white lie.

"All dressed up like that?"

Ernesto hesitated to answer and was immensely grateful that Dad did not pursue the subject. He wondered if there had been a hidden motive for the probing question, whether there was more to come, whether he now knew about his girl and was this his way of saying so, or whether he disapproved and let it be known in this manner. Whatever it was, it did not feel good, but a single thought of Hanna made it all worthwhile. He felt himself walking the fine line that separated the deep roots tightly attached to staunch family conformity from independent wings of freedom.

A friend from work had invited him to come over with Hanna. Ernesto felt so great about his girl that he needed to share his pride with someone. Not knowing exactly how the potential union was being received among the rigid immigrant community, he resorted to his native friends. In typical Latin fashion, Marco was listening carefully, giving accolades based solely on description, and immediately displayed his duty of hospitality and invited Ernesto to bring her over. It was the first invitation the two had received. It was something to celebrate and be proud of. Sure, it was an extra-community invitation, but it was a beginning. The rest would surely follow in due time.

She sat on the center bar of the bike as he pedaled heroically. The friend lived in an area not served by busses and Hanna had thought it would be fun to go by bike. Pushed by the wind, her white dress described the shape of her legs while she clung to the handlebars as the bike negotiated the uncertain terrain of the eroded dirt road. The experience was another discovery along the road of shared love. Both enjoyed it. He was happy to have the strength to propel them both and being able to suppress his heavy breathing enough to avoid having to reveal the major effort. Her natural athletic coordination made this a wonderful balancing act for her. The road went into a decline, giving Ernesto the needed respite. As the bike clicked into high gear so did their glee. With his legs spread far from the pedals, he let out a shout of enjoyment. Their ringing laughter echoed into the neighborhood.

"Muy buenas noches, adelante." The welcome was sincere.

Ernesto hesitated for a moment as to how to introduce Hanna. The choice of words would have as much significance to Hanna herself as to Marco.

"Mi amiga, Hanna." Ernesto glanced over to her and saw her slightly downward tilted head with upturned eyes and a wonderful smile. Her dimpled lip shone beautifully. She was pleased and Ernesto was happy.

"Adelante, mi casa es su casa." And indeed Marco seemed to mean it as he brought chairs and invited them to feel at home. Marco's cavalier attention went to Hanna both because she was a beautiful lady, and because she was the guest just introduced. He wanted to know of her work, her origin, her feelings about the city, whether she missed the country, whether she liked the music, the food, and on and on.

"Does he take good care of you?" Marco suddenly asked, as he pointed to Ernesto.

With a flash of embarrassment that temporarily flushed her face, she replied, *"Si."*

Marco served a drink from a bottle. After sipping a bit, Hanna realized it was not the wine she had assumed, but a sampling of the strong *caña* distillate. She pushed the glass over to Ernesto, who not only finished his, but also forced the remains of her glass down his rebelling throat—and still managed to steer the bike home without incident.

9

The old Ford pickup sped along the narrow road heading east into the countryside. This, the only black topped road in the entire country, seemed to stretch like a long black band, which through gravity had found its lowest level among the hills and forests. Where no ·vegetation stood the red earth stretched far on either side, accentuating even more the intenseness of the black road that already seemed out of place with its smoothness among the gully-scarred countryside, bearing evidence of frequent torrential tropical rainstorms.

Much planning time had gone into this event and now they would soon reach their destination: the mighty Iguazú Falls. The lead pickup was packed with happy youth full of anticipation. Several vehicles brought the rest of the group.

It had been a stroke of luck that Ernesto and Hanna were seated in the front cabin next to the driver. He did not remember how it had happened but it made him eminently happy that the driver had invited them to sit there, as it surely was a seat of honor. He liked the feeling of sitting up front in lead of all vehicles. He liked the tightness of the cabin, sitting close to Hanna with their body sides paralleled inch for inch from legs to thighs to shoulders. He liked to see Hanna wear his hat. It had happened while they were waiting for the caravan to start on its journey. In her playful manner, she had teasingly stolen his hat and run with it. Pursuit was obvious, but recovery was not. Eventually he had given up and she had joined him with a conqueror's smile. Ernesto took pride in her physical abilities. She wore his hat for the rest of the day.

The driver stepped hard on the brakes and swung across the road to avoid the cattle, which had suddenly taken a left turn from the meadow onto the road. Hanna and Ernesto braced with both hand on the dashboard. The change in position gave Ernesto an excuse to now put his arm around Hanna as they returned to a normal sitting position. Not much was said as both pursued their thoughts. It had been rather nice to be the first to get those choice seats and to see dozens of young people as they passed the pickup cabin to find their seats. A few of them had stopped and teasingly shaken Ernesto and Hanna's hands as though congratulating, some even whistled, some just smiled. Someone had even wanted to take a snapshot of them sitting in the pickup. Playfully Ernesto pretended to block the camera, but someone had held his hands back so that the photographer could take the picture. Somehow, it appeared that the Hanna-Ernesto affair had just gone public—officially. Nice.

"Documentos, por favor," was the icy request from the military police officer. He seemed to be doing his job with such inflated sense of self-importance, and was quite successful in creating a quiet air of nervous fear among all passengers. Normal chatter resumed the minute the control station was passed and the beautiful rolling hills once again continued undulating by.

"Everybody quiet, please, quiet." The youth leader struggled for several minutes to gain the attention of the excited youth.

"Now, I want you all to know that we stopped here on this hill and turned off the engines so that we can listen for the distant sound of falling water. So everybody listen quietly."

An awesome feeling overcame the group. It was a far sound, but unmistakably the sound of something huge and foreboding. It announced majesty on the grandest scale, something to behold, the mighty power of nature at work.

The remaining miles went quickly as the distant roaring sound became louder and more intrusive. The first of the falls made its appearance. Bordered between countries, the mighty falls would likely have been labeled one of the natural wonders of the world had their access been easier at the time such contest took place. The two and a half kilometer thunderous semicircle harbors 275 different cascades, some with 800-foot falls—a much greater falling distance than found in the Niagara Falls. The names of the various cascades are as awe-inspiring and mystical as the falls themselves: Devil's Throat, Adam and Eve, Three Musketeers, Two Sisters.

The youth group leader shouted one more warning: "Be careful, everybody. Don't get too close to the edge. Remember, the ground is slippery from the mist and the moss. Stay on prescribed paths only. You are free to explore for the next hour."

Ernesto and Hanna went to explore this mightiest of all water works. The deep roar was overpowering and intimidating.

"Did you know that many people have lost their lives here?" His voice had the ring of instruction.

"What did you say, I can't hear you," she shouted.

"I said that this is a dangerous place, where many people have lost their lives."

"Do you suppose they slipped and fell?" she yelled over the roar of the falls.

"Yes. Who knows how many people have gone just a bit too close. And maybe they were not even too close, but a sudden gust of wind pushed them off balance and down they went." Ernesto was now standing very close to her.

"Look at all those crosses. I wonder how many there are?" She pointed to the white markers along the precipitous edges identifying accident sites.

"During the period of the Spanish conquest, the Jesuits came to this area to establish missions among the Guaraní Indians."

"I bet they had a tough time getting through to them."

"Not only that, but once they got to the Indians, many Jesuits were martyred using the very symbol they brought to the mission."

"What do you mean?" she asked.

"Their symbol was the cross. Often the Jesuit missionaries were killed by tying them to a wooden cross, which was then dropped into the stream far above the falls. If lucky, the cross stayed right side up with the missionary, tied with arms spread, floating down river and his face gazing up into the sky as he prepared to meet his maker. Speed soon picked up and the cross eventually plummeted down the vicious waters, carrying its human cargo to certain death from either pounding impact or drowning in the gurgling waters."

Ernesto and Hanna backed off and went exploring further above the falls. A path through the dense, dripping tropical forest took them up some steep inclines only vaguely reminiscent of steps. They negotiated the treacherous moss-laden rocks by hanging on to each other and to the many jungle vines, which seemed to reach out their skinny arms from all sides. Life along the path bubbled with vitality. There were only short periods that rains did not fall. Plants seemed to have developed the ability to absorb water from the constant spray using a miraculous osmosis mechanism developed in their leaves. The greens were greens of the intensest nature; the reds and yellows and blues of the flowers could only be matched by rainbows, sunsets, and skies. Even the aroma of the flowers was intense and distinct. A *toucan* bird above croaked its funny song, calling attention to its colorful plumage and immensely oversized rainbow-striped beak.

Eventually the path led to an opening above the waters. A narrow hanging bridge stretched high above the rushing waters seemed to beckon exploration. The spray-soaked faces of the two young explorers shone with excitement as they hung on to the guide ropes and carefully ventured onto the bridge. It was an excitement propelled by the definite element of risk. He watched Hanna in her tight slacks walking forward with such apparent carefree and sure-footed movements. As she so often did, she had taken the loose ends of her shirt and tied them into a knot, thereby exposing a belt of mist-soaked, bare skin. The stormy roar below, the feeling of floating in the mist on the waving bridge, and the threat of possible disaster seemed to heighten his passion for this splendidly erotic female before him. This was the girl he loved. All the energy of his manhood called for her. As she proceeded forward, Hanna stopped occasionally to glance back to see if he was still following.

The hanging bridge opened to a wider section above the middle of the rushing waters far below. Ernesto looked at the waters below in terror, then he gazed at the smiling, mist-soaked girl before him. With both hands, she hung on to the rim of the hat to keep it from flying over the edge pushed by those unpredictable gusts. Beads of mist slowly made their way down her forehead to the eyebrows, onto the nose, and finally her earlobes where they hung like glittering diamonds. With fun in her eyes, she cupped her lower lip, tilted her chin heavenward, and sent a stream of breath to her nose to free the sparkling drops. This laughing, lively creature, which had been raised in the jungle and matured now with a definite wild disposition, seemed to feel so at home in these tempestuous surroundings.

He approached her, slipped his hands around her bare, wet waist, and pulled her close. He moved his hands and forearms back and forth feeling the skin of her stomach, fresh with youthfulness and warm with life. His arms seemed to melt onto the contours of that sensuously slender waist. He turned her toward him and drew her closer, and for a long time fed his eyes on her red mouth, which seemed to bud as succulently as a fresh fruit. He kissed her cheeks, tasting the saltiness the spray had dissolved from her skin. But then suddenly, as though driven by impulse he pressed his lips hard onto hers. The deep, long kiss brought wholeness to their beings. In contrast to the cool spray, the salty taste, and the great roar of the waters below, the kiss felt warm, sweet and secure—everlasting. It was the taste of merging joys. The powerful Iguazú Falls seemed to applaud vigorously.

Arm in arm they walked back to the park for the picnic. Ernesto's thoughts involuntarily went to his parents. *Might they approve of her? Certainly they, as everyone else, could see her beauty—there could be no doubt about that. But do they know how nice a person she is, how totally feminine her disposition is? Might they object that she is not educated and refined in cultural diversity?* But certainly they would recognize the fact that such things are secondary and can be acquired, whereas beauty and love are the gifts from God. Certainly they would want his and their happiness, and such incidentals as book learning would certainly be excused. Might they talk to him about her? Did they even know of his love for her? He wondered if he should be talking with them to diffuse any possible misconception on their part. No, the authoritarian father figure did not encourage heart to heart talks. *They will like her!?*

Holding hands, they moved along sharing a beautiful secret—a secret that was natural and simple.

The picnic was in full progress. It was a joyous time. Ernesto and Hanna were inseparable. They walked hand in hand or they put their arms around each other's waist. They inhaled the air perfumed by scented flowers, spoke with friends, and ran into the meadow. At times Ernesto was not sure he could distinguish his Hanna from the beauty of the flowers or the zest of the flowing stream. The forest, the sunglow, the butterflies all seemed to be transfigured to a likeness of Hanna. They sat in the meadow and she leaned her elbow onto his lap. He watched her peel an orange and lick the dripping juice off her fingers and then explode with radiant laughter. All her actions seemed to fit together. She touched him lovingly and seemed to say, "I'm yours." They took photographs of each other, of themselves, and with others. He loved the way she tilted her head forward slightly as though protecting her eyes from the sun. The so uplifted eyes made a marvelous picture. Ernesto's sister, also a member of the youth group, wanted to be photographed with Hanna. Ernesto took that as a sign of approval from home—and oh, how good it felt!

The trip back to the city was again filled with laughter as happy youth sat tightly packed in a pickup truck shouting their untrained voices at top volumes singing familiar folk songs.

"I'll see you in the morning?" he teasingly asked once again, as he dropped her off at her residence.

"You silly goose, you know we both have to work tomorrow."

"Oh, that's right. So when will I see you?"

"I'm afraid not until Thursday evening—you know that."

He gave her one last kiss and said—in jest—"I'll see you in the morning." She smiled, waved him off, and closed the door.

Ernesto skipped down the road whistling a happy tune.

10

The voltmeter read 6.2 volts for the filament of the tube suspected of malfunctioning. Leaving the black lead on the chassis of the disassembled radio, Ernesto moved the red lead to the anode. The voltmeter read the expected 240 volts. Keeping the radio chassis set on end with the underside and its hundreds of connections exposed, he returned to the diagram to study and continue the search of why the radio did not function. It had become obvious in the last fifteen minutes that the problem was centered on this particular vacuum tube. *Could it be that the grid is the problem where there is a resistor and a condenser connection,* he wondered to himself. The expected voltage was not there; in fact, there was no voltage at all.

Armed with the hot soldering gun whose tip had been cleaned by dipping it into rosin, he removed both the resistor and the condenser. *The absence of voltage would likely not indicate a flawed resistor, since it would only break a connection, but it might be in the condenser, which often shortens out, thereby rerouting the current to the ground.* His reasoning proved correct, and replacing the condenser returned the radio to its proper functioning.

Ernesto loved the work at the radio repair shop. Not only did it provide some income, but it provided a challenge to his intellect and, on successful ventures, a boost to his ego. Most repairs were detective ventures into the realm of electronics. With experience he became more accomplished and the correspondence course on electronics helped even more. It was a good feeling to see three or four repaired radios lined up at the end of the morning. It felt good to be in command of the knowledge and vocabulary of the trade. And it felt even better when, on occasion, he was called out to the homes of the city's elite to consult and repair their elaborate sound systems.

His walk home for the three-hour *siesta* break always had an extra bounce to it when the search for the flaw of the inner workings of a radio had been long and hard, but the solution had been found. Soon the sharp, orange smell of the burning rosin from the solder gun tip became associated with the sweet smell of success. He carried that smell in his nostrils far from the repair shop.

On his way home, he liked to sit on a bench in the plaza and enjoy his feelings. The perennial shoeshine boys surrounded him with their pleadings of *lustre, lustre, señor?* The noon crowd criss-crossed the plaza in search of a mid-day resting place. He saw the stately buildings all about the plaza housing offices, banks, businesses, and even vaults containing the bodies of glorious heroes. As the shoeshine boy tapped his box, thus calling for the next foot to be placed on the box, Ernesto wondered about the wealth surrounding the plaza and the half-naked boy at his feet earning a few *centavos,* which he likely depended on for complete survival. He remembered the many speeches he had heard as a student, marching along endless parade routes during the ever recurring national holidays celebrating ever so detailed a heroic event in the history of the country. Dignified speakers loved to hear themselves talk about the country's proud past, which seemed to increase in feat and fire from year to year. They spoke about the accomplishments of this city of the *conquistadores,* the heroism of its founders; but speakers skillfully failed to acknowledge the decay and poverty all about.

But then his thoughts became more self-centered. He was particularly happy this week since Hanna had come to visit him at work, and he was able to impress her with the detailed intricacies of the job. He had been conscious of the personal time he took during her visit, being careful not to make it too obvious to those in command that she was a friend, not a client. Yet still, as always, he was proud to be seen with her and took every opportunity to introduce her to fellow workers.

It was on one of those warm tropical evenings that he went on a planning mission to The Angel statue. He had always enjoyed walking about its upper platform or going down its dozen sets of steps, each landing on a large platform perfect for strolling about. It was a quiet area since vehicle traffic was blocks away and those with business on their minds avoided the steps. During the day children played, racing up and down the steps, and during the evenings it seemed to be a favorite spot for couples in love. It was a perfect spot to let the imagination go, to take in the wonder of the city lights below, and to inhale the fresh breeze from this high vantage point. It gave a feeling of being in control, above it all—a feeling of omnipotence. On either side of the steps luscious and varied vegetation seemed to provide ever changing colors and aromas. But perhaps best of all was the sculpture of the angel perched high up on the solid column at the top platform. The Angel was draped in a gown that seemed alive in the breeze. Pointing heavenward it reigned over the area spreading love and peace to those below.

Ernesto had often observed the couples along the wall or sitting on the steps. They appeared to have found the ideal spot; they were at peace and so happy under that angelic eye. He had come this evening, alone, to plan a future visit to the area with Hanna. He liked the spot on the upper platform to The Angel's immediate right. It provided a most beautiful view of the city below and the harbor with its passing ships in the distance. It also afforded the closeness to The Angel, which subconsciously he hoped might bring a blessing.

And it was on the next date that he and Hanna spent a happy hour under the wings of The Angel. They leaned their bodies over the waist-high retaining wall and absorbed the tropical evening. For a long time they watched the ships in the far distance trek across the bay. The Maria Angola bell from the Cathedral below once again spread its soothing sound like a blanket over the city. Couples in love meandered about on the platforms below, swinging their clasped hands up and down in a carefree manner. Somewhere off in the distance someone was plucking at a harp. Ernesto broke a branch ablaze with blooming flowers off a nearby bush. Placing it in her folded hands he removed one flower and slid it into the waves of her golden hair.

Theirs was a love of wildest happiness. They were made whole with boundless joy. They loved because everything around them willed it: the trees, the city, the lights, the air, and, yes, The Angel above. Ernesto spoke the only word when he whispered "Hanna" through the curtain of her blond hair. To him it was the word of ecstasy, the word that allowed him to lose himself in the delirium of joy. It was the word that freed him to just let go as demanded by passionate love. It set a fire ablaze, racing through the veins within him. Both felt the excitement made possible only by entry into the primitive and subconscious kingdoms of lover's souls.

He turned to admire her face. God's handiwork was indeed perfect. Her mother-of-pearl white skin gleamed in the evening light—in competition only with her fleshy red lips so full of expectant life. There could be no sweeter taste than the long passionate kiss they engaged in with her arms around his neck and her hand buried in his hair. Standing next to her, and his heart racing with the speed of burning passion, he placed his right hand on the bare round of her shoulder, exploring its tenderness; his hand then felt the warm pulse of her throat, and then, slowly, daringly, his hand lowered itself in exploration to find the young fullness of her breast. Showers of tingling sensations swept them both as he began to enjoy the contours of soft firmness. The next few seconds were to have a lasting impact on his life. While he had attempted to explore the next horizon of love, she gently, yet firmly, took his hand and held it in hers. She seemed to be saying: "Let's not mar our beautiful love. We have so much as it is. Let's not do anything that could destroy our love with guilt. Let's continue being happy lovers." It was the only advance of this nature he was ever to make.

Ernesto wanted to shout for joy. He was immensely proud of her. She had stood up for her principles, she had taken a risk, and she had done the right thing. His respect for her jumped by quantum leaps. He wanted to announce to the world: "Look at this beauty in body and spirit! And she is mine!"

He took off his coat and hung it over her bare shoulders to protect her from the cool evening breeze. Remaining behind her with his arms tightly around her waist, he inhaled the freshness of her hair as he pressed her softness against his tall, muscular body. For the first time he felt the entire length of her slender body molded against his. Up and down his lean body he sensed the outline of hers, every curve, every narrowing, and every soft spot. He felt a body alive, giving off warmth and vigor. *Is all this really for me? I am rich!* he thought to himself. *If there is truth on Earth, it must be revealed in this feeling.*

The Angel became a favored spot of theirs many times during the months that followed.

That night, Ernesto got home late, as he often had during the months of courtship. Due to the advanced hour of the night, the front doors were locked and he had to use his key to the large iron gates to gain access to the yard. From experience he had learned how to very carefully turn the key so as not to make much noise, and then ever so slowly and carefully swing open the heavy gate. He had to keep it from belching its metallic grinding sound, which emanated from un-oiled hinges, into the late night and thereby awaken the parents. He bit his teeth in an unconscious effort to avoid hearing any sound possibly created. All went well until he walked to the house where his father materialized from the darkened hall and announced:

"We'd like to talk with you."

His heart skipped a beat or two, and then sharply increased its rhythm. Given both the hour and the circumstances he knew this would not be a pleasant conversation that fate held in store for him. He knew that it certainly had to do with his dating, and likely with Hanna specifically. He knew that neither his father nor mother had ever said a direct word about the subject, let alone indicated any sign of approval. The subtle hint he had received from his father on that walk to church about being known by the company one keeps, now suddenly seemed about to evolve from hint to admonition. Given Herman's persistent pestering and his parent's occasional hints, Ernesto no longer had to suspect their stand. On the other hand, it was not common for parents to talk to their children about matters of the heart. Perhaps they would see the real girl that he knew. Perhaps they were going to talk about the fact that he had, in recent months, neglected his reading of the many good books available in the home library.

Sitting uncomfortably in the dimly lit room with his parents in their nightgowns, he waited.

"We'd like to talk to you about that girl you seem to be dating."

That sentence abruptly brought him back from what had a half hour ago been an ecstasy of the far shores of love.

What do you mean "that girl"! he wanted to cry out. *Don't you know who she is? She is my Hanna, a girl of superb integrity—if you only knew! And what do you mean "seem to be dating?" We've been going together for nearly a year now and our lives are one.*

Father continued in that same solid voice. "You must remember that we are all known by the company we keep. And our place in society is often determined by those with whom we associate."

He had heard that line before. His thoughts flashed back to the time when he was in third grade. Maria had been an intriguing girl to him—as intriguing can be to a boy of nine. She was in fourth grade and thus socially somewhat out of reach, nevertheless there were occasions of group get-togethers where she was also present and he could feed his young imagination. On one occasion, being desperate to get her attention, he had slapped her face lightly with the back of his hand. The slap itself was playful enough, unfortunately, however, one of his fingernails hit her eyeball, causing pain and tears, and for Ernesto, trauma. When word got to the parents, the punishment was a severe spanking. It somehow imbedded in him the certainly false connotation that in his father's eyes, girls were to be stayed away from. The subject of girls had never been discussed by his parents; in fact, they did not even engage in gentle teasing, thereby giving the feeling so needed by growing boys, that "girls are okay."

Father was still talking. Ernesto thought he heard him say something about the need for compatibility. Ernesto was both angry and numbed. The huge lump in his throat and the Old Testament edict "Fear your parents" made this a totally one-way conversation. As he struggled with his feelings, he heard Father continue speaking but, again, he really was not listening. Ernesto thought he heard him say something about her being a maid, about her not having finished high school, about how important it is it be educated, and about how much they as parents had sacrificed to provide their children the opportunity to study. The indication was that she was from the "other side of the tracks." Once released from the clamp of the preaching, he went to bed exhausted.

Never again would his parents bring up the subject. They never spoke of her, and to his knowledge, never spoke with her, and never did they provide even the slightest indication of approval. Fighting back tears, he wondered why it was possible that something as beautiful as a true love could possibly be oppressed by the powerful forces of societal disapproval. To thrive to its fullest, love must be nourished by parental blessings, the approval of friends, and the applause of the community. Love wants to share of its happiness. It wants to shout to the world, not hide. Yet, apparently Hanna and Ernesto were not to reap such blessings.

Ernesto felt that their courtship had now gone underground. While at one point he might have dreamed of her inclusion into the family, he now became withdrawn and secretive. Proper society events, banquets, weddings, theater attendance, and the like, he attended alone, or if possible, not at all. The pain of exclusion drew him ever closer to his love. And their love grew ever stronger as though reaching for the stars. It was a love of determination, a sharing of common pain, one experienced only when love is opposed. *Why does something beautiful reach its highest pinnacle only under severest stress and tension?* he wondered.

The emotional highs and lows, the deep pain and the exalted joy were physically tiring experiences. He slept long and often. But one thing was clear: He was not giving up his Hanna. He could not wait for the next date. With Hanna he did not share his pain, only his joy.

11

The old bus rumbled along filled beyond capacity, causing its mass of compressed humanity to flow back and forth swinging in unified resonance with the contours of the rough road. While the passengers inside quietly struggled to breathe, the chickens on the roof, with their legs tied in bunches, noisily protested their fate. Stopping at every intersection more passengers were pushed into this human compactness with shouts of encouragement to "move to the back, there is plenty of room."

As the kilometers agonizingly moved by, the countryside mellowed and quieted as it became increasingly freed of the burden of population and its abuse. Cars gave way to *carretas,* the tall, two-wheeled ox-drawn wagons that have been the means of transportation since the days of the *conquistadores.* Slow and cumbersome, these oversized Roman-style vehicles are nevertheless reliable and versatile, having transported goods and people for centuries. The vast plantation fields of pineapples now began to give way to virgin forests, where trees owe their towering strength to the rich earth and gracious rains. Eventually, the bus reached the intersection at the Botanical Gardens. Relieved, Ernesto and Hanna exited.

Nature had dressed the park in its spring best. The green meadow, the blossoms, and the butterflies all appeared to be in color competition. The sounds from insects and birds filled the air. Most astonishing though was the huge sea of trees in white bloom. Every green leaf on every branch on every tree was surrounded by an explosion of white flowers. It seemed that the ocean of white spread in all directions, gently undulating in the afternoon breeze. The heavens were filled with the aroma of the flowers and the sound of bees seizing the abundant gift.

They had come for a private picnic and to be a part of the wonder of it all. At the sight of the expanse of white, Hanna stood in awe for a moment as her eyes swept in all directions. She set down her basket, and with her hands on her back leaned against the trunk of the nearby tree. She stood there for a long time with her chin up and her eyes closed, eagerly inhaling the freshness that engulfed her.

Suddenly she raised her arms and ran into the midst of the whiteness. With her head thrust back her hair bounced in wild rhythm. Her feet, as though on springs, seemed to give her body freedom from gravity and allowing it to float like a butterfly. It was the sight of a carefree creature blending into her natural surroundings.

Abruptly she stopped at one of the trees waving her arms as if chasing something away. She turned and motioned for Ernesto to come.

"What is this?" she asked, pointing to the two little jerking pouches hanging from a point on the underside of a branch.

"Those are cocoons or shells, the pupa stage of the creation of a butterfly," he said, catching his breath.

"The birds were eating them and I chased them off. Only two are left," she lamented.

"Notice how they are moving in a flip-flop motion. They are trying to rid themselves of their shells."

"Why is it so hard for them? Why did so many get destroyed by the birds? How long will it take for them to come out of the shell?"

"Sometimes it takes long, sometimes just a few minutes."

As they watched the metamorphosis happening before their eyes, one pupa slowly broke its shell, and there, before them, hung a young butterfly from the tip of its wings. And soon the other burst its shell as well. Both hung motionless from the exhaustion of birthing.

Ernesto and Hanna sat down to watch and protect the two new creatures. They felt happy, overwhelmed by a sense of youth and robust health. Everything about them, below them, above them, and beside them seemed saturated with life. Their lives, too, became new as their souls became one. They had no thoughts of the future, only the now.

Within a few minutes, the hanging butterflies began to move slowly at first, then shake and flip vigorously. In an instant the pinned wings were miraculously freed, the released butterflies seemed to fall for an instant, but then spread their wings and took the first flight. Two pairs of radiant wings flapped hesitantly against the blue sky.

"I'll race you back to the picnic basket," she challenged, and was off in a high-speed dash—naturally arriving first. While waiting for

Ernesto to catch up, she made another running circle and then collapsed on the ground laughing mockingly.

Her open, panting nostrils quivered with life as her bosom rose and fell, paralleling her heavy breathing. This creature of the wilds obviously felt at home. Her dazzling beauty was enhanced by the beads of sweat that emerged, sending forth vapors of good health. She displayed the carefree spirit of a child, the free will of a beast, and the beauty of a woman. Her eyes were definitely those of a woman in love. For Ernesto the inviting smile from the virgin freshness of her lips became irresistible as he claimed her mouth... The oneness they experienced was God's way of revealing to his creatures a glimpse of heaven.

She closed her eyes and suddenly thought of a time long ago, processing impressions that had crowded her life ever since she could remember. She could remember back to about 1944 when life appeared to have some kind of routine in that village of theirs in South Russia.

She remembered mostly happy times. Sharing a room with her older sister was fun because she could watch all the things big girls did and had and talked about. She also liked playing with Katja, the neighbor girl. They spent many happy hours in the orchard—just pretending. They built cities and houses in the sand. The streets were laid out just like the ones for their own village where people were farmers and had beautiful horses. But what they liked most was playing house. Their dolls were brought out into a pretend room under the apple tree to feed and clothe them, to take them on walks, and to instruct them as mothers must do. As in their own families, the dolls also had no fathers. They were not quite sure where they were, but they must be on a job far away. Maybe they would come home sometime. That would be strange. She wondered where Katja was now and whether she was happy. She wondered if her mother had been this happy when she courted her father.

Winter had been special, she remembered, because people stayed inside more and built a fire to keep warm. Somehow she did like to be close to the kitchen where it usually smelled good and inviting, especially after she had been outside with her brothers skating on the pond. Her older brothers were good to her, often letting her come along and do things with them that her older sisters were not allowed to do. Maybe it was because she was the youngest, or maybe because she was too small to fight with them.

Mother had always admonished her to finish all the food on her plate. That would have been okay if the food had not always been the same beans. It seemed there was always talk about food in the house. She worried that maybe there would not be enough someday because she had heard her mother talk with her brothers and they said something about shortage and famine. Sometimes after a meal she would go out to the orchard and try to find some fruit to eat. But she did not really like to do that since she remembered eating green apples one time and getting really sick.

She remembered Mother sometimes crying and then talking about Daddy. This happened either when she had been over to Katja's house for a visit, or when she just sat by herself. The older sisters would then quietly sit with her. She remembered one day the entire family was scared when some men rode up and talked very loud in Russian. Her brother said they wanted horses. There was only one mare in the barn, but she was really too old to do much work. The rough men went to the barn, but did not take her. Later that night there was some shooting on the other end of the village. She had a hard time going to sleep because horses were galloping up and down the street and her mother and brothers would not go to bed, but they had the lights out and did not talk. She thought that was strange and somehow it made her frightened.

Ernesto watched his sleeping beauty with admiration. He marveled at the creator who had sculptured such a masterpiece. Her facial lines were soft and graceful, yet already had an aura of determination springing from the unfairness the world had sprung on her young life. Her untamed character made her all the more irresistible. It seemed impossible to have a purer happiness than the innocent love of these two hearts here surrounded by the blue sky, the odor of the flowers, the hum of the bees, and the taste of pineapple.

Her life had changed his. Her aliveness, her exuberant spirit, her vitality, her native intelligence, her quick wit, and her beauty all had awakened within him creativity, optimism, strength, and purity of motives he had never known before. Her person had catalyzed in him the drive and determination to achieve, to persist; she had awakened the urge to tackle, to lead, to perfect—all attributes that were to serve him so well on the road for the rest of his life. She had given the supreme gift a woman can give to a man by calling out the very best in him. She had lifted his spirit heavenward. He thought, *How could anyone doubt that gift? How could anyone imply that formal education, which is such a recent social phenomenon, is really necessary? Necessary for what? For show? Is it not the human spirit that is ultimately important?* Hanna had given Ernesto a gift he was to keep forever.

On the way home from the Botanical Gardens they sat in happy silence in that noisy bus, nourishing their thoughts. After a long time she broke the silence.

"I received a letter from my mother. Our family is making plans to migrate to Canada."

The lines on his face stiffened and a grim expression settled about his mouth. He could almost hear the pounding of his heart onto the rib cage. He wanted to say something, but the lump in his throat was too heavy. He took her hand in his and they sat in silence.

Reverend Isaac had stopped Ernesto before the church service asking to see him after church. The preacher did not normally talk to the youth unless the subject was of ominous importance—like the several times he had stopped him to inquire about Ernesto's plans for baptism and church membership. Ernesto had thought about it. At nineteen, he probably should consider doing the proper and expected thing in this community believing in adult baptism. So maybe the reverend wanted to do some more gentle persuading.

"How are things going with you, Ernesto?"

"Fine, Reverend Isaac." Ernesto wondered in anticipation what the next line would be.

"Ernesto, I have been thinking about you. You know, you are growing and maturing, becoming older and interested in more things, new horizons. This is the time in your life when you have so many options and many new decisions are made. For some young people it is almost too many decisions at once."

101

Ernesto wondered what this was leading to, whether his parents had spoken to the Reverend, and whether this conversation was about to turn to the subject of girls.

"Most decisions that young people make at this time have life long implications. Schooling, profession, when to leave home, all are important questions. And so is the choice of a life partner."

So it was concerning his courtship, after all.

"Do you know what I mean, Ernesto?"

"I think so, Reverend."

"You see, when two people get together and become more serious, they must ask themselves many important questions. Will the love that they feel now sustain them through the rest of their lives? When beauty fades, are there other compatibilities that will form a solid foundation of their merged lives? Do they have similar heritages, beliefs, and aspirations? Do they have the same cultural and educational background and values?"

Somehow, the conversation became more and more reminiscent of what his father had been saying. Was this a set-up? He became agitated.

"Reverend, are you talking about Hanna and me?"

"Well, I am just wondering if you are thinking about these broader questions."

The disapproval shone ever clearer through the hints and insinuations. How was this possible? Except for a few youth group members who had made teasingly pleasing comments about his relationship with Hanna, no one else, certainly no adult, apparently favored the union in the making. He could not see why society seemed to be so obsessed with disapproving. Was this not a matter between two people and between them only? How could anyone else know, really know, what they felt and thought?

His thoughts went back to the movie he had seen, alone, quite some time ago about the young Austrian nobleman who fell in love with a beautiful girl from the ranks of commoners. He enjoyed the beautiful love story, and ached with them in their pain of society's other expectations. Their love grew ever stronger as did the demands of the royal court to give up the girl. Ernesto remembered the intensity of devotion they showed for each other and the commitment to die, rather than live apart. Facing an ultimatum from the throne,

102

the lovers had made their decision and retreated to a secluded room. The haunting sounds of Johann Strauss' *Kaiserwaltz* were soothing as the movie focused on a solitary swan gracing a lake. Suddenly the peace was broken as a pistol shot rang from the nearby room, then a second shot, and then silence. The swan swam away.

Ernesto withdrew, not only from the uncomfortable presence of the preacher, but also from social events, from his parents, and from the expression or any hope of celebration of his feelings. He had an uncharacteristic thought about the line for his eventual epitaph, which he decided he wanted chiseled into his gravestone reading: "He was touched by true love."

It was Christmas time. They exchanged small presents and each was to travel to attend separate family gatherings. A special present to themselves was a studio photograph of the two of them—he dressed in suit and tie, and she in a dazzling white strap dress that highlighted the youthful color of her skin. Their complexion was clean and fresh. Her wavy, shining hair encircled her young face. She tilted her head toward him. Their expressions were innocent, solemn, and seemed to convey a distant pain...

After taking her home late that evening, he walked back to the trolley stop. At this hour, the trolleys came few and far between. He sat down on a nearby wall and waited when he heard the sound of a familiar motorcycle. Yes indeed, there came Herman whose economic position was such that he could afford personal transportation. Many times he had met him somewhere in the city and had always picked him up for the ride. All it would take for Ernesto was to flag him down. It would have been a quick ride and could perhaps even avoid any possible unpleasant confrontation at home. But Ernesto also thought of the inevitable conversation that would take place on the way home when Herman would probe and question and tease and imply. Ernesto did not want to ruin his good feeling from the evening with Hanna. He stepped behind a tree to avoid being seen. The sound of the cycle came closer, then passed, and fainted into the night.

During their short separation, he missed her unbearably and she was constantly on his mind. Once reunited, they resumed their happiness with a certainty to ever be lovers. She casually related the attention she had received from young men in her home community. She would not confide in him the extent of that attention. This produced in Ernesto a turmoil of feelings: pride that she was obviously being noticed for her beauty, and jealousy of potential competition. It was definitely a streak of fickle character of hers that yielded strong reactions. Such hard-heartedness could only erect barriers.

He chose not to continue probing for details but was in desperate need of affirmation. He sought to erase his doubts of loyalty in things small and great he observed: her gifts, her organization of his picture album, her attention to his doings, and simply her presence. Was their increased passion perhaps fueled by the thought of a triangle? Was she something less than he knew her to be? Heaven forbid!

As he picked up their pictures from the studio, he noticed that a large one of them had been prominently displayed by the studio in the picture window facing the street, there for all to see. Obviously the photographer was proud of his professional work and it felt good, but what if the wrong people would see it? There would be new trouble! Unwittingly he thought of the time he was in second grade and on a Saturday afternoon had found entrance into the one-room school. While playing on the blackboard, he had accidentally dropped and broken the only long piece of chalk so cherished by the teacher. The rest of the weekend had for him been agony as he visualized possible impending punishment for his sin.

12

Neither of them really knew quite why. Why were they going to Ernesto's home? Never before had Hanna been there. It had always been an unspoken understanding to avoid that which was not accepted. And certainly his parents had not accepted her, had never spoken to her, let alone invited her to the house, so why were Ernesto and Hanna now going to his house? Even Ernesto could not really place the reason for the visit, except that he felt an urge to do so. It was a need, a longing to fill something incomplete. Hanna had agreed to it—on the way to the movies—but she did not understand the reason and was apprehensive about it. Sure, Ernesto had timed the fulfilling of this urge to bring her to his home very carefully: his parents were gone, so it would be safe.

The closer they came to the house, the quieter they became. Ernesto felt her presence on his right. He sensed her beauty, the youthful grace of her body, and the spring-like fullness of her body. The sincerity and energy of her passion converged in his imagination and made him happy. Why did she not seem acceptable to some? She was so full of vivacity and bubbling spontaneity—free to laugh, carefree in thought, and happy in actions. Could it be that this natural spirit was misunderstood as being pompous, loose? Certainly not, if she was just given a chance to be known. Perhaps there was a certain jealousy in others as they observed her beauty, grace, and happiness. Would she consider the discipline of intellectual endeavors? Certainly she had the ability to do so, but would that be a bribe for acceptance into the upper crust of the immigrant society? That should not be necessary. Human beings and their relationships should be accepted for what they are.

Ernesto and Hanna walked along the cobblestone street negotiating the unevenness of the sidewalks, which seemed to have been laid for the convenience of the builders rather than that of the pedestrians.

At the front door, Ernesto carefully inserted the key and slowly turned it in its lock. He entered with investigation, checking for signs of unexpected life.

"This is the living room, here is my dad's study, and this is where we eat. The kitchen is down the hall." They slowly explored the house.

"And where is your room?"

"Down to the left."

As they entered his room, Hanna's curiosity was obvious as she surveyed the surroundings. Ernesto's face drew serious as he watched her and his thoughts seemed to go somewhere far off.

He thought of the encounter he had had some time ago with the Reverend. Ernesto still was not sure what the real purpose of that uncomfortable discussion had been, but he did know that approval it was not. It seemed contradictory. On the one hand, the spoken words from the pulpit were of love, understanding, acceptance, and equality for all, yet the lives of the parishioners did not really live it. After the church service, visiting groups formed not only along age lines, but along acceptance lines as well. While two persons might have been sitting next to each other on the pew during services, they may have briefly acknowledged each other's presence, but after services, unless of the same social strata, would bypass each other seeking out their equals—equals in accomplishments of the mind, culture, the use of everyday vernaculars, work, and relation to the native population. It seemed so trivial, yet so deep-seated, perhaps unconscious: a discrimination which had been brought along from Europe.

Ernesto focused his thoughts closer to his circle of friends. Herman was his very good friend, he liked him and the feeling was mutual, yet Herman did not approve of Hanna. It was understandable since Herman had tried for a long time to awake in Ernesto amorous feelings to one of his many sisters. True, Ernesto had shown some interest in one of them, even had a few pro forma group dates with her, but the fire never kindled. So, Herman's disappointment was understandable. What about his other friends like Jake, John, or Rudi?

"What in the world is this?"

Ernesto's thoughts were brought back to the room as he saw Hanna curiously pointing to a picture on the wall.

"Oh, that is supposed to be a self portrait. You know I like photography. One day I decided to take a picture of myself. So I had to pose and at the same time reach back to release the shutter. That long reach and the awkward angle are reflected on the grimacing expression on my face. So that's what you see."

She giggled in delight as she continued her survey of the environment.

Why had Rudi not congratulated him on this beautiful creature of God's making? Like the rest of his friends, Rudi was a student, spoke in proper High German language, had professional ambitions, and therefore was a member of the unspoken, invisible acceptable layer in society.

"And this? What is it?" She pointed to a picture on the wall depicting a young girl with a somewhat sad look and a tear on her cheek. He had taken that picture out of a yearbook

"I don't know anything about it. Except that I like it. I don't know why I like it. Perhaps it is the suffering that seems to be implied on the young girl's face. Perhaps it is the title of the painting: *Undeserved Punishment.* Maybe that is how I feel."

Suddenly it struck Ernesto why he had wanted to take Hanna to his home. It was the deep felt need in his heart to seek his parent's blessings. In his mind, he knew that this was not to happen, and in fact he had chosen to come home at a time when they were absent, and he had avoided ever talking to them about her. Yet while his mind spoke reason, his heart longed acceptance.

He imagined they would be sitting in the living room with his parents engaging in small talk. At one point his father would say: "Hanna and Ernesto, I'm happy for you," and Mother would embrace Hanna. In this whirlwind of confusion between the mind and the heart, he hoped that the physical visit to the house might perhaps bring the hope of a blessing closer to reality. He thought of Jacob in the Old Testament who, being nearly blind, was tricked into blessing his younger son when he thought he was giving his blessing to the older son. The confusion, the impossible hope, and the desperateness all filled his soul beyond capacity.

"What is wrong, Ernesto?" Hanna asked, as she saw him crying quietly.

He took her into his arms, held her tight, and let the sobs vent the feelings. Nothing really mattered to him. He was not interested in things, books, school, other people, relationships; he only wanted her to be with him. All of life's experiences were measured against that sole wish. He did not care where he was to be, or what he was to do in life, as long as it was with her. Yet, to make a formal proposal to her seemed so impossible.

Hanna sensed the struggle and kept her feelings in her heart. While happily in love, she refrained from bold overtures that might further cement an impossible joint future in this layered society.

13

"Do you love me?" he asked, as they once again stood under The Angel. All over the entire firmament, the twinkle of a million stars in red, and amber, and yellow glow seemed to compete for attention. High above them the constellation of the Southern Cross reigned majestically. It lay on its side, as was the case during most of the night. Instinctively Ernesto checked the southern direction. His father had taught him, a long time ago, how to use the Southern Cross to tell which way is south. You take the long stem of the Southern Cross and extend it downwards three of its lengths by following its direction—no matter how the Cross lays. Then, at the end of three lengths, come down in a straight vertical line to the horizon. That is always south. The ancients had used this technique to aid in their navigation and travels. Ernesto looked down and saw Hanna's white arms glowing like those of a goddess.

She did not answer his question verbally. He often wished she would show more directness of expression. Her non-responsiveness gave him concern. Was it aloofness? He wished she'd say "Yes." It made him try even harder to conquer her, if any conquering was left to be done. When she smiled at fellows who paid attention to her, he felt a jolt of jealousy. Was she flirting? Why couldn't she just say: "I love you?"

No, she did not answer verbally, but never before had the color of her face been so lovely. It mirrored a love anchored in the depths of the soul. It transcended warmth, affection, and tenderness. It was an irresistible fascination. They had become true soul mates. Their love had released them from their separate selves, immersing them into a union of solid oneness. Someday, many years later, that feeling was to return.

It was the night before her departure for Canada. That event was so momentous in both of their minds that neither understood it nor spoke of its impact. They drowned that incomprehension in total devotion to each other. He put his coat around her shoulders and in so doing, locked her in his arms. They stood there for a long time watching the quiet city below.

It was a beautiful, cool spring evening. A light breeze had cleared any feel of humid stickiness from the day. Fresh flowers had opened from what the day before were only buds; nightingales flew silently through the air catching their prey.

They found a nearby bench where they sat silently for a long time, numbed by the events about to happen in their lives. Neither knew the future but for now, they just enjoyed the pure beauty of togetherness.

"Do you think the moon shines as beautiful in Canada?" Ernesto wondered. Hanna said nothing but enjoyed his voice.

"Hanna, you are mine, and I don't care what anyone says or thinks, you are mine." They turned to kiss as they had so many times. Fueled by fear of the unknown, and of impending separation, they felt their souls uniting ever more. Ernesto touched his girl by the shoulders, gently turned her so as to lay her head on his lap. Her wide, sweeping white dress covered the bench and playfully described her body shape. What a joy to touch those exposed shoulders. He felt the firmness of her young flesh and the shape of her arms molded by a God who clearly knew supreme beauty. Her succulent mouth protruded invitingly like a budding flower.

Clasping his arms around her upper body, he drew her up from his lap. With her arms around his neck, she responded with an indescribably soft embrace that seemed to say, "Yes, I am yours."

Ernesto's mouth came crushing down to hers, demanding possession. He felt the fullness of her lips; they were warm, wet, eager, and ready to meet his. The embrace locked tighter, the plundering kiss grew intense and long, riveting two lovers together. At last they seemed to be able to express what words could not: "Events are taking us apart, but we are one." The kiss continued, seemingly stopping eternity in the midst of angelic happiness.

He whispered sweet nothings into her ears, surrounding her soul with mystery thus increasing her desires. Hanna signaled in yet a new way that, "I am yours." Her tongue began to slowly move as though searching. The feeling brought new heights of sensation. Then her tongue found its destiny as it slowly penetrated his mouth. Ernesto kissed it, drew it, and caressed it with his. No one had ever told them life could be so beautiful. Now his tongue penetrated her mouth, was received with womanly gentleness, then it returned in tandem with hers. The anticipation of continued joys tensed their insides, and neither knew where their body ended and the other's began. Back and forth, back and forth as in an innocent, harmonious dance the two tangled tongues seemed to be driven only by instinct. His lips became hers, and hers his.

With happy glee, Hanna threw back her face exposing the softness of her neck. It was an invitation to kiss freshness. Then in symphony they opened their mouths to once again plunge into carnal oblivion, desperately seeking to exploit the well of unspeakable happiness.

Only occasionally did the kissing stop; their lips red and swollen to firmness by the impact. They did not talk. There was no need. True friendship comes when silence between two persons is not only comfortable, but beautiful. Hanna and Ernesto found a love made in heaven.

"I'll see you in the morning," Ernesto finally said, thinking of the noon flight she was scheduled on.

"That'll be nice. Yes, and this time it will have to be in the morning."

It was late when Ernesto returned home, having made arrangements to pick her up in the morning for the trip to the airport. As he undressed for bed, he realized a strange wetness. It was new, but felt right.

Some six miles away, as she prepared for bed, Hanna, too, had discovered a wetness, though not new for her. Still, it made her feel so womanly on this, her last night in the tropics. Lying under the sheet she put her arms beneath her head and watched the setting moon through the window. She could feel the wholeness of her body. Her mind sensed the shape of her feet, legs, torso, and arms. She could feel her firm breasts and erect nipples thrusting into the sheet. Her body was well, alive, and in full bloom. Hanna's somewhat sad smile radiated hopeful happiness when she finally fell asleep.

At the airport, they sipped sodas, took last minute pictures, and strolled the halls. Ernesto even took the bold step to speak with her

111

mother, and say farewell to her brothers and sister. Then it was time to part from her who had given him new life. A new life with new reasons to live. She had instilled in him the desire to work hard, to drive toward perfection, to serve others unselfishly, to make this a better world, to glorify her. Her womanliness had called out in him the manhood he was meant to experience.

They faced each other for the last time. One more time he looked into those big blue eyes, sparkling like sapphires imbedded in a sea of tears.

"I'll see you in the morning?" he asked, playing their little pretend game.

She nodded and smilingly responded in a broken voice:

"Yeah, I'll see you in the morning." With his curved index finger, Ernesto wiped off the tear that ran down each of her cheeks.

Then he watched the big silver bird take one half of his life into the northern skies. While destiny took their bodies apart, their souls would remain one. Little did either know how fate was to lead their lives.

He was now twenty, and she was eighteen years of age.

14

Destiny appeared to be smiling on their lives. Upon arrival in Winnipeg, Hanna soon found a job and spent her energies on her work. Ernesto returned to his work and self-improvement studies with renewed vigor and purpose. He enrolled in a correspondence course and spent many evenings studying the intricacies of electronics. His young mind was eager and able to absorb complex theories with ease and delight. Driven by the synergy that comes with success, he spent many hours assembling electronic devices and would smile exultingly when they worked. Once again, he found the time to nourish the ties of camaraderie with friends of his boyhood. But he tended to avoid Herman. "Is she still writing to you?" he would sneeringly ask, and sarcasm would drip through his teeth. It was reason enough to avoid him.

Ernesto and Hanna corresponded heavily. She related the excitement of the Canadian world and the activities of her kin. He reported newsy items, his work, and his longing for her.

But destiny smiled most graciously on them when it became clear that Ernesto might have a chance to go to the U.S. for studies. And in fact, that opportunity became a distinct possibility, and before long it was reality. Excited by the event, the love letters darted north and south with increased frequency.

Ernesto had much to do. There were the documents to prepare, passport pictures, passport, health certificate, chest x-ray, visa, tickets, and college admission. His few belongings needed to be disposed of. Some were sold, others stored at home. He sold his voltmeter for $50—the only money he would take to the U.S. His employer gave him a good letter of recommendation. All systems were set to go.

The departure from family and friends was hard. It was clear to everyone—though no one said so—that this would be good-bye for a very long time. It was the close of one chapter and the beginning of a new one. As he walked the tarmac teary-eyed to the waiting plane, he stopped to send a last wave. It was a good-bye for his family and friends there gathered.

But the depth of the feeling sprang from the realization that this was good-bye from his native country, from a culture he had grown to love, from familiar surroundings, from an ease of familiar languages, and from the tropics. But most of all, it was a farewell from the cradle of his youth, the place where he had fallen in love—for the first time. He left behind a time and place where he had experienced the mighty power love has on young hearts. It was that power that had instilled in him what was to steer the course of his life. That power had told him: "Go out and do well, conquer the world, compete, rise to the top, and make her proud of your achievements, make yourself worthy of her." He was both sad and glad. Sad that those tenderly innocent years lay behind, glad that he now had a chance to fulfill those urges of striving—and glad to be nearer to the source of that awesome power.

The plane finally landed in Miami on a hot day in July of 1959. Ernesto's energies were consumed adjusting to the unfamiliar culture and language. A three-day bus ride finally deposited him at the college nestled among the amber waves of wheat. The next eight months were to be an emotional tug of war as new impressions and old feelings penetrated him from all sides.

There was a new language to learn, housing to secure until the new school term a month later, and above all there was a job to be found to finance the upcoming expenses. It was all so strange and unfamiliar. The efficiency of one's activities that comes with familiarity had been left some 6,000 miles to the south. Now every act took extra effort and energy, caused by the sheer newness of his surroundings.

It couldn't have come at a better time. It was one familiar experience; it was a link to the past and held hopes for the future. It suddenly renewed in him the most intense of all human feelings.

Her first letter to his new address arrived on a Saturday noon. It was the only mail item and lay in the mailbox in such a way that the return address was visible through the tiny mailbox window. Written with the familiar blue ballpoint pen, there were those long awaited initials H.V. followed by the address and Winnipeg, Man., Canada. Winnipeg... the name had taken on mystical meaning in Ernesto's consciousness. That was the city that harbored his love. Since arriving in the U.S., he had often looked at a road map studying the route that led to that city of his thoughts. Calculations showed that it would take a long day's drive. But he might as well have been in Siberia. He had no access to a car, and even if he did, he had no money for the gas. Without means or friends, he felt a prisoner on the open prairie.

His fingers quickly ran through the combination to open the box, but in his hurry missed it and had to start over. Her letter was a happy one—she always seemed happy and carefree. What was lacking in grammar was made up a hundredfold in enthusiasm for life and her typical hints of love. It seemed that her letter lifted their common soul high upon a pedestal.

Ernesto's day took on a whole new aura. While he went through the motions of painting an old porch, his thoughts were elsewhere being reunited with his soul mate. He reread her letter a dozen times. It fueled his existence in those strange surroundings.

Evenings were lonely times. He desperately needed her. He needed her exuberance, the closeness of her body, the touch of her hand, but mostly he needed to talk with her. He used to imagine that she would come to visit, that they would sit in the dorm lounge and talk, walk down the tree lined alley past the tennis courts to the open field. They would begin to talk about their future—something they really had never done much of. Perhaps, so he thought, she would come and get a job in town and maybe take a course or two. Perhaps she'd even like it and go to school full time.

All were conversations in the mind of a yearning, lonely young man. His letters transmitted some feelings, but certainly could do no justice to the whirlwind of thoughts in his mind and feelings in his heart.

Letters continued to travel north and south with predictable frequency. While Ernesto was interested in every sentence, word, and syllable, he nourished his soul most completely on the expressions of love. Those expressions were usually not the common "I love you," but rather were given indirectly, almost teasingly. She had a knack for implying love by what she said and how she said it. She did not take love for granted nor did she impose it. This veiled approach kept Ernesto's desire piqued, on edge, and forever fresh. She knew how to play the careful balancing act between a love taken for granted and aloofness. Particularly he liked the many ways in which she would sign off her letters: "Your loving Hanna," "Yours forever," "Your ever remembering friend Hanny," "Your baby," "I'll see you in the morning."

With the beginning of the new school term, still another set of completely new experiences catapulted upon Ernesto. The campus was filled with new faces and sounds. Enrollment, books, tuition, lack of funds, roommate, jobs, classes, and fear of failure all demanded a place in his repertoire of thinking and feeling.

The requirements were many. There were classes to attend, a language to learn, there were laboratory sessions, studies, a totally unfamiliar use of the library that everyone else seemed to know, etc. Furthermore, several part time jobs were necessary in order to pay the bills. What little cash he had brought along was quickly gone on basic winter necessities, leaving him with but a lone nickel in the drawer for the remainder of the term.

Yet a new experience was the presence of so many bright fellow students who posed a real challenge to compete with. Then there were the quizzes and exams and the inevitable resulting disappointments.

Rest and repose from the new hecticness came in the form of the letters from Hanna. They provided roots, shared love, and brought boundless joy. Occasionally she enclosed a photograph of herself. He noticed she still favored white and it was still so very becoming. He looked at these treasures a thousand times.

His parents also wrote often. Despite all their support and encouragement for his studies, he felt as though the letters from them and those from Hanna came from vastly different—even clashing— worlds. The parents expressed their joy and admiration for his presence in college; Hanna expressed such pure joy for life itself. Instinctively he even filed the letters in different places. He wondered if the two disparate worlds could and would ever meet; if he could earn their approval of her. Perhaps if she came to college…

College was a stimulating place. Surrounded by intellectual and artistic talent, the mind and the spirit soared freely to explore and expand. Ernesto reveled in the opportunity to be a part of the world of thought. New worlds of knowledge and unheard of talent exploded before him. Once, while doing his janitorial chores between classes, he noticed a student playing the organ. Her demeanor was studious, her attention focused. What amazed him most was the incredible talent brought to fruition in such a young person. It spoke of years of study and self-discipline. Ernesto continued to push the mop as he pondered. Could all girls learn to do that? His parents certainly would have offered such training to their children, had it been within their means.

That week, Hanna wrote the most ebullient letter about her outing on a lake. He could almost hear her laugh as she talked about running on the sandy beach. She included a picture from the beach and spoke of her new, shorter hairstyle. Ernesto wondered if those beautiful smooth waves of her hair were now gone.

He felt trapped. He desperately needed to talk to his Hanna. There were so many things happening which he needed to tell her in person—not by letter. Yet he was trapped in a place he could not leave. He needed to process his feelings and impressions, and most of all he needed to hold her to renew love. He also felt trapped without anyone whom he could confide in and check feelings with. He did not want to lose her, but was afraid that time, distance, and continually mounting separate experiences were not helpful. Should he make a bold move and propose marriage and let educational ambitions take second place? What about his documents? He was on a student visa that he would lose if he discontinued his studies. Would it even be possible from the government's point of view to just stay?

They had never talked about marriage before. Neither had felt the need then, since their love kept growing stronger with each contact. But now, they were separated and he was fearful of what might come. He was sure she was receiving plenty of overtures from fellows in Winnipeg. If they were to get married, how could they possibly manage without aid from anyone or the possibility of a loan? Would she even consider leaving Canada? He just had to talk with her. Should he take the ultimate risk, drop everything, and hitchhike north? The turmoil threatened his equilibrium. It was a lonely struggle fought by a lonesome student who had no one to share his grief with.

His parents wrote about new books they had read, illustrating their letters with thought provoking quotes. Particularly they again recommended Norman Vincent Peale's *The Power of Positive Thinking*. It lifts the mind, they said, to heretofore unheard of heights. The limits of achievement are set in one's own mind.

College life, both in and out of the classroom, did indeed become more and more stimulating. Recitals, banquets, football and basketball games, homecoming, fairs, all were enrichment opportunities totally new to Ernesto's experience. It was from a detached distance that he observed the dating process the American students used while attending these various functions. He noticed the common college experience these couples shared, which seemingly always gave them an abundant source of conversation.

Hanna wrote describing her sister's wedding. In fact, she enclosed a picture of herself as bridesmaid. For a moment, it let his imagination soar only to then quickly become mere wishful thinking. The picture displayed her radiantly in her white dress. In that so very characteristic manner of hers, her head was tilted forward slightly, her big blue eyes peering upwards and her glance seemingly supported on wings of a heavenly smile. That was the Hanna he remembered. Just then he needed to hold her, touch her, and kiss her. He wanted to see her run in her carefree way. Her spirit of freedom had always lifted his spirits and placed him above any woes and toils of the day. But oh, it had been such an eternity since he had seen her. Why must it be so??

And the college experience continued to be challenging and exhilarating. It was demanding of time and intellect leaving little chance for the mind to wander into wish land. Studies also proved fun with all the new methods of teaching and learning. Insights into discoveries came abundantly. Being of analytical mind he had never thought that literature and poetry could be presented and understood, or felt, in such a spine-tingling way. He marveled at the beauty of the colors in the chemistry laboratory, the cohesiveness of the law for the standing wave, the need for balance between mind and body as exemplified by the importance of sports. College was indeed a place he wanted to be.

The months went by. Propelled by a restless mood, Ernesto took a bold step and asked a girl on campus for a date to attend a banquet. It felt strange to be in the presence of another woman. For a moment, a curious sense of freedom overcame him; but it was quickly subdued by feelings of guilt toward Hanna. Was she perhaps also suffering from this interminable separation? Was she accepting dates? Certainly she was surrounded by many admirers. Her beauty and outgoing happy-go-lucky attitude made her so utterly attractive, vulnerable.

Ernesto thought about that ancient legend he had read a long time ago. It held that in the beginning of time mankind was asexual: every person was a complete and whole entity needing to relate to other persons only for business and communication purposes. But then mankind sinned and the High Spirit separated each and every person into two parts. Thereafter all new beings were born as half-persons constantly in search of their missing half. While several combinations of halves could match to complete the person, there was, for every being, only one opposite half able to make a perfect match. Mankind's struggle and pain is to find that perfect match. The boundless joy is to have found it and to be whole again—to be of one soul. Hanna, he had thought, was the perfect match for him.

His parents wrote that his friend Herman had married Gerda. Ernesto had been jealous of Herman, not because of Gerda, but because of the attention Gerda received from his own parents. Obviously, she was to their liking: she had studied nursing, spoke High German, and had a good job.

It seemed that the letters traveled less frequently between Canada and the U.S., were shorter and less intimate. As the months rolled by, Ernesto had a few other dates for college functions. Something did not feel right. On the one hand, he did want to be part of the college social life, which included at least an occasional date. True, there were only a few such dates since they had to be arranged around his heavy work schedule. On the other hand, he wanted to remain true to his first love—but how could the entrapment of distance and time nourish that love? How could the parental high expectations, now so clearly reinforced by the college environment, how could these always pounding reminders of "oughts" and "shoulds" be successfully counteracted if no strength could be drawn from a constantly reassuring love. Letters helped, but he needed to hear her voice, see her face, hold her hand—yet there appeared no hope in sight.

But just then he received another most touchingly beautiful letter from her expressing her belonging to him. More than ever he was torn, uprooted, bewildered. He needed to talk, but no one would understand. In desperation he sat down one evening and wrote Hanna that he did not see their lives coming together in the foreseeable future, and that therefore they should perhaps terminate their relationship. He had performed an act of the mind and in the process, stabbed his own heart. He had done what was reasonable and expected of him. The mind said "yes," but the heart shouted "NOOOOOOOOO." He sealed and stamped the letter and then held it for a few days. One morning, in a reckless moment, he mailed it and then went to class. Henceforth, and for the next forty years, all his decisions would be primarily cerebral and logical.

Instinctively he took all her letters and pictures, carefully arranged them in neat order, tied them together, and put them away in a safe place.

"I broke up with my girlfriend," he said to an acquaintance, whose only response was "Oh well." He wanted to talk, share his sorrow, check his decision, receive affirmation, to be consoled. However, that two-sentence exchange would be the only processing he would ever do—until forty years later.

That week he happened, once again, to sweep the floors of the music hall. Among the students practicing was that girl he'd seen weeks ago on the organ. This time she played the piano. He was even more mesmerized by the beauty of the sound and the agility of her hands, which danced over those keys without any apparent effort. How was it possible that the same person who played that mighty organ could also play the piano with such ease? As she walked out, he noticed the erect and stately posture with which she carried herself. Her clothes were proper, her demeanor high. Certainly she belonged to the campus elite. *What a cultured society this is!* he thought, as he gathered the pile of dirt into the dustpan and proceeded to repeat this same task in the next room.

Like an alcoholic who buries his problems in drunkenness, Ernesto launched into an affair with a local high school girl. Here were two young people with vastly different backgrounds and values—but who were both in need. He needed a means to forget and push into the back of his consciousness the doubt and sorrow of his first love. He tried to erase completely the space his first love had occupied in his life and then sought to allow a stranger to fill the void. In the desperate search for new love, he only found shallowness. Whitney, on the other hand, was in demand of all that wild love could yield in order to have her amorous needs fulfilled. For a brief time they provided each other with the expected service, and thus fulfilled their separate needs.

The impossible trap he found himself in would permanently twist the fate of his heart. Yes, he was to love again, but not a first love of irresistible and totally giving passion. He would love again, yes, a love of expected matrimonial domesticity, a love common and accepted by society. But the love of the fierce fire that burns to total consumption, that blind first love could be given by and to only one.

And so, in his aimless search, he returned for a time once again to the innocent unruliness of adolescence, when first love had not yet wounded him with its sweet poison.

Riwen Forester

Interlude

Riwen Forester

And the proper love affair did come. It was an expected relationship with the girl who had mesmerized him with her piano and organ playing. They had the proper dates going to college functions, banquets, and the local symphony. She introduced him to choirs, choruses, and chorales, grand operas, mighty organs, piano music, larger-than-life symphonic orchestras, oboe solos, the Messiah, majestic requiems, good books, and museums. She would go on and earn her Masters Degree, and became a good, loyal, professional wife, providing decades of normal married life.

Ernesto did get his Ph.D. and settled into the routine of daily life, with a major university appointment, teaching, research, promotions to full professor, administrative appointments, publications, three children, church membership, building a solid financial base, attaining power and influence, and doing all the good and expected things in society. Always driven, he never felt that he had arrived, spent his time getting ready to live, and yet did not seem to have enough time to live.

Their marriage was good, but the daily routine, where stability becomes more important than happiness, pushed back romanticism. They seemed happy in public, but were sometimes aloof in private; lacked the carefree openness needed for intimacy; and some differences were kept to themselves, with each partner pursuing his own right.

He traveled a lot, and while his travels took him all across the U.S., South America, Europe, and the Far East, he never went to Winnipeg. Over the years, Ernesto visited his homeland and often he also went on walks to Avenida Santísimo Sacramento and to The Angel, sometimes wondering "what if." But it was not until some forty years later that these fleeting thoughts would suddenly be replaced by a stomach-turning avalanche of emotions triggered by a set of blue eyes belonging to a colleague who had just arrived from Winnipeg.

Hanna's life, too, evolved in the expected Canadian way with a flash-fire romance, marriage, family, job, friends, and a routine that dulls the senses. Initially she often thought about Ernesto, and then less so; however, for forty years she always thought of him on the first of the year, his birthday. But excitement was rare, and the drudgery of daily life was numbing.

It was on one of those days, when the hours pass in a predictable manner, that her mother called, as she often did. But this call was different.

"Would you do me a favor, Hanna?"

"Well, of course, Mother. What is it?"

"I want you to take me someplace."

That was not unusual for Hanna to take her mother on a trip. Marta had always taken care of the family, had gotten a job when they first moved to Winnipeg, but then had slowly eased off as all got older. She had never learned to drive, plus she was advancing in age, and of course, she had no car. She lived in a self-contained unit of a nursing facility not far from Hanna's home. So, a request to take her someplace was not unusual. Hanna did not mind taking care of her mother. What was unusual was that there seemed to be a bit of secretness about the request.

"Mother, where are we going?"

"I'll tell you later, when you pick me up."

It was not like her mother to be secretive about things. She had always shared her innermost thoughts with her children—after all, she had no husband to share such things with. So, it was with just a bit of apprehension that Hanna went the next morning to pick her up. She went into the nursing home, turned left to Room 15A.

The piano was playing. It was something Marta had begun doing once again. For so many years, the family had no piano. It was too expensive, too cumbersome, too out of place with the tropical environment they were living in. But here in Winnipeg, after many years of work, after the children were established, and she, too, had reached a level of comfort unheard of for so many years, she was able to acquire a piano. To be sure it was used, but once properly tuned it played well. She was able to get some of the sheet music she had been playing in Russia, and in the long evening hours was to again go back to the days of Russia, the days of her youth, and through the piano relive the aristocratic life her father had once provided her.

After listening for a few moments, Hanna knocked on the door.

"It's open, come in… Please, close the door behind you."

126

Hanna sat down and, contrary to her normal chattiness, she waited. Her mother stopped playing, turned herself around on the piano bench, and looked at Hanna.

"Hanna, do you remember when you were a child, before we moved to Winnipeg, I often told you stories about Russia after our chores on the little farm were done."

"Yes I do, Mother."

"Well, I don't know if you remember, but once I did tell you about someone by the name of Aaron Tilitzki. Do you remember that?"

"I am not sure. You told us so many stories."

"Well, in any case, he was some 15 years older than I was, he was a business partner of my dad's, and came on visits every two or three months. I remember him coming to our house ever since I was a little child. Somehow, I became infatuated with him when I was but a teen. I don't know if he ever felt the same for me, but he paid attention to me—perhaps just as a friend. I was his friend, the child of his friend, but to me he was... well..."

"Mother, that was a long time ago. What about it?"

"He moved to Canada, long before we moved south. I lost track of him, but this last year I did some checking. This week I found him, and he lives here in Winnipeg. He is in his nineties and I do want to visit him."

"Whoa! Are you serious? How did you find him?"

"That is a long story, but I did find him."

"When do you want to visit him? Is that where we are going?"

"He is expecting me today."

It was a quiet ride across town to the retirement community where Aaron Tilitzki lived. They pulled up to the parking lot, walked to the reception, and a bit awed at the luxurious surroundings, asked for Aaron Tilitzki.

"Yes, just go down this hall to suite *Lake Winnipeg*." It was a courteous reply from the receptionist.

"Hanna, I want you to stay here in the waiting room until I come and get you. I want to meet him by myself. There is so much we have to catch up on. Please?"

"Of course, Mother."

Marta walked down the hall, passing suites with all kinds of names. In her mind, the long hall seemed to transform itself into the estate gardens in Russia her father had tended so carefully. She could feel the warm hand Aaron had given her as they crossed the newly dug trench so long, long ago. That day she had become a woman— she had acquired a new feeling about herself, about womanhood. Now, she was about to meet him again.

His door was ajar and she knocked lightly. There was no answer, but she could see a piano in the room. She pushed the door open, slipped in, and sat down to play. Not many chords into Beethoven's *Moonlight Sonata* she sensed his presence somewhere in the room. She continued playing, but then stopped and looked around; and there in front of her, erect as always, stood the man, now in his 90s, who had helped her see herself as a new being. They stood there a long time, just looking at each other. Then Aaron reached out his arms toward her and they embraced. They embraced for what seemed an eternity, for indeed it had been an eternity that had separated them. He could feel her crying quietly. He unlocked the embrace and wiped the tears rolling down her cheeks.

As he closed the door he said, "Here, please sit down."

"Thank you."

"How in the world did you find me?"

"That is a long story. But I am glad I found you." Marta surprised herself with her honesty.

"How are you? Last I heard from your father you had gotten married. That was ages ago. How is your husband? How is your family? Do you have children? Are they grown? Are they here, too?"

They had much to talk about and they did so for a long time.

But then, Marta suddenly changed the subject,

"You know, Aaron, your visits to our estate were always fun for me. I always looked forward to your coming. I think I was in love with you."

"I suspected that. And I was attracted to you, too."

"Whoa! So, why did you never tell me? Why did you move away?"

"You were, and still are, 15 years younger than I am. I felt you needed the experience of youth finding and loving youth. I was no longer youth, though it would have been easy for me to get closer to you. Perhaps that was also part of the reason why I moved."

"In a way that is a bit sad."

They sat there in silence for a long time wondering about what ifs.

Then Marta reached into her purse and withdrew something. She gave it to Aaron.

"Here, open it."

"What is it?" He was genuinely surprised to get something.

As he unwrapped the tissue paper, the Russian wooden vase revealed itself that he had given her many decades ago. He remembered its delicate shape, its relatively heavy feel, and the intense black background onto which brightly colored leaves and fruits were painted.

"This is amazing. How have you kept it so well all these years?"

"You told me to keep it for something special. After we left Russia, I did not have many special things in my life, but your memory has always been special. I kept it for that."

They embraced and he kissed her lightly on her forehead.

"My daughter is waiting in the lobby. Can I bring her to meet you?"

"Well of course. I'd love to meet her."

He called down to the desk and gave instruction to have her come down. It was just a few minutes until Hanna was at the door.

"Aaron, this is Hanna, my youngest. Hanna, this is Aaron Tilitzki, a very special person in my life. I knew him from Russia. He was my first flame." Had she had a second chance, Marta might have taken that back.

"I can tell, Mother."

"How can you tell?"

"I am a woman, I can just tell."

They all laughed.

Riwen Forester

Part III

I'll See You in the Morning

Riwen Forester

1

It had been a particularly busy Monday thus far this March 13. Mondays were usually busy at his business, TSS, but it seemed to Ernesto that his secretary had allowed the schedule to become unduly full. Upon arrival he had, as usual, first met with his staff to go over the plans for the day and the week. During such times, Ernesto was particularly proud of John, his chief of staff. John had opened the meeting by pointing out the negative effects of the tax law changes, and the slowly rising interest rates. But, in typical fashion, he had already made tentative plans—pending Ernesto's approval—to dispose of some properties and begin to search out new acquisitions, particularly from among those investors who were only looking at quick, short term gain and tax write-offs. They now would be ready to sell, at a loss if need be.

Ernesto sensed that John had grown into the position of chief of staff with ease and confidence. He seemed to always have a very plausible proposal to possible difficulties.

By nine that morning, Ernesto found himself immersed in negotiations with a group of Japanese investors eager to spend their money, but wishing to use his expertise. Ernesto liked their courteous manner and it helped to know that they came with cash. They made a tentative agreement to invest 49% into a shopping center Ernesto was considering. He would control business decisions, but they would retain the right to sell anytime, provided that a) they gave TSS first right of refusal, and b) that they give three months notice. This was a tactic used many times before to give new investors confidence in TSS. Ernesto knew from past experience that they would not exercise these rights because he trusted his judgment and intuition, and would be sure to make the venture a success.

Ernesto left the conference room and returned to the office. To his surprise, Jane did not stop him with messages or reminders. He closed the door behind him and sat down looking at his speaking appointment calendar. During the next talk, he wanted to use the just finished deal as an example of sound professionalism. From his

133

calendar, he saw that he would have many opportunities to talk about the venture.

The phone did not ring and his eyes wandered about the spacious office. *It really is nice,* he thought to himself. *The paneling, the couch, the heavy oak desk, the bookshelves, the awards.* Now, in his early sixties, he had accomplished much.

"Life has been good to me, and there are so many more opportunities." He said it out loud as he pondered the just finished deal. His eyes fell on a copy of the second book he had just completed, *The Source of Success.* It had brought him still more recognition from the business community and, even more than that, he enjoyed the other by-product: the frequent lecturing engagements to business groups and universities across the country, where his books always sold well after his presentations.

In fact, he was now considering a series of tapes and CDs from his past talks. If packaged and promoted properly, they would also sell well. He had written the book like he did so many other things: It was done over and beyond the normal duties. He had been able to do it in a relatively short period of time because he was well organized. He had taken the broad perspective, and then fleshed it in with many useful and detailed ideas. He was constantly collecting ideas. While driving, flying, sitting in meetings, his pad was always handy for quick notes. At night, he would occasionally wake up with a sudden idea or the solution to a troubling problem. Those bits and flashes all became the substance for fleshing out talks, papers, and books. Reader response had indicated that it was these little things, the tables of facts and specific hints that so many people liked in his book. He knew he could do likewise with the tapes and CDs.

Jane called at 2:45 pm. "Dr. Bauman, remember the reception you have at three."

"Do you suppose I can skip it?" he wondered aloud.

"I don't believe you should, sir. Remember, the foreign visitors will be there, and we have invited all the new company employees. They are expecting to see you." Jane sounded insistent.

"Do I have to make any remarks?"

"Only if you want to. The main thing is to be there for a few minutes and meet and greet people."

"Okay, I'll go for a few minutes."

Ernesto moved through the crowd with the ease and confidence of a man in charge. "How are you?... Give me your name, please.... I hope you'll like it with us." The many years of such pleasantries made them natural.

What happened next would be over in a few minutes, but would leave his life utterly changed forever. A new employee introduced herself.

"Hi, I'm Sharon Horton-Classen. I just joined TSS a few months ago."

"Glad to meet you. I'm Ernesto Bauman."

"Yes, I know," she said. It happened often that he did not know people who knew him.

"Where are you from, Sharon?" The question was perfunctory.

"I just moved from Winnipeg."

She was a middle-aged lady with energetic and vivacious blue eyes, but otherwise bore no resemblance to anyone from his past. Yet suddenly, an avalanche of feelings erupted from within, bringing to his consciousness she who at one time, a long time ago, had been so important to him and his life. He could feel his heart pushing into his throat. As with a bolt of lightening, he remembered forty years back.

He had been in the process of nibbling on a cracker. Unable to consume it, he laid the broken cracker onto the table, but kept his hand planted there firmly for support. He feared he might faint. As she spoke about her life, he kept looking at the blue-eyed lady, who now had no importance to him other than that she had been the catalyst for a strange awakening. His eyes gazed upon that unfamiliar face, but his inner eye beheld a beautiful creature from the past. The lump in his throat was about to choke him; the dryness of his mouth and the emotions pounding his heart against his rib cage were all strange feelings, yet only seemed to grow as the minutes passed. Somehow, remotely, they were not new sensations after all.

Forty years ago he had experienced the same sensation when tormented by the dilemma he felt between attraction to Hanna's beauty both in body and spirit, and society's unspoken other expectations of him. Somehow, in the ensuing forty years, the deep down feelings had apparently not been vanquished, but had been waiting as if in a dormant volcano. The lava had crusted over but now the entire mass had burst open.

Ernesto felt flushed. His eyes popped and his ears were buzzing strangely, becoming hot. He did not recall how he finished the conversation with the blue-eyed lady, but in a half-daze and with labored breathing, he found himself stumbling out of the room and into his office. He felt that a long-forgotten virus in his system, after lingering for decades, had suddenly come to life and was now eating on him with disregarding ferocity.

"Mr. Johnson called several times. You need to sign these letters, and you promised you'd call your wife before four," were the greetings from Jane.

"Not now."

"But, these letters are urgent."

"Not now. Please, cancel all appointments."

"Excuse me, but what about the salesman who just flew in from Atlanta because you promised an appointment?"

"Not now!" He firmly closed the door behind him.

2

He threw off his coat and loosened his tie. It was terribly hot in that stuffy office. Like a pierced animal, he paced up and down, then suddenly stopped in front of a chair and gripped its two armrests. He squeezed it, almost feeling the wood yield to the power of his grip. The sweat from his forehead dripped onto the leather seat and his confused feelings gave way to uncontrolled shaking.

In his mind's eye, he saw Hanna in all her youthful beauty; in his heart he felt her vigorous life, he saw her gracefully fluid body movements, he felt her soft touch, and he heard her carefree laughter. He saw the girl that long ago gave meaning to his life. She was there in front of his mind's eye, in all her glory.

What is this? he thought to himself. *I have all I want, a good family, a successful profession, so what is the matter? I did not seek this rediscovery of a past love. Why is this happening?*

He constantly kept wiping his forehead and his neck. They were drenched. Ernesto changed the thermostat setting to cold.

He realized that slowly he was losing control of what was happening to him. Was it his conscience speaking; was it repentance, pity, worry, or just a biological change in his body?

This surely must be a passing thing; I haven't heard a thing from, or about her in forty years. Certainly, I appreciate beautiful women, but this is crazy. His thoughts continued to race.

He made a quick mental inquiry. Had he been thinking about Hanna? No. When was the last time he had thought about her? He could not remember. He thought about his many trips, his long absences from home on business—were those times when he thought about her? No. How about during the early 1960s? All inquiry yielded the same no. Over the years, he might on occasion have thought about her—as he might have about any other acquaintance from his past. Such fleeting thoughts likely would have come during visits to his country of birth when familiar surroundings bring to mind past experiences. He had no idea if she was alive or dead, and, if alive, where she lived, what she did. To him she had, until an hour ago, been so distant she might as well have been dead in Siberia.

The torment had lasted too long. He could hear the phone ring on the secretary's desk, but she was doing her instructed duty.

Then a new frightening feeling made its presence known. He remembered from his psychology studies that persons later in life often revert to original habits, likings, languages, and patterns of thought. *Does one really go back to that which was originally implanted in the heart, the consciousness, and the mind? And is the return most likely to those things which are fundamental in life—first impressions, first family relationships, first instincts, and, yes, first love?* His questions had no answers.

Aren't all feelings God-given? If so, what is the meaning of this? What must I do? What I can't and really shouldn't have, I now suddenly think about and feel? Why, after forty years? Who should I speak to? No, I better not tell anyone!

He walked to the window whispering, "God, help me; forgive my feelings—no, no, thank you for my feelings!" His eyes gazed empty into the distance as his forehead, nose, and lips were pressed flat against the cold glass pane.

Ernesto left the office early that day. Passing the staff, Jane gave him a timid look, while others worked quietly. Only his chief of staff attempted a hesitant, "Are you all right?" Halfway out the door he replied, "I'm fine," and was gone.

The fresh air in the parking lot did him good. He could smell the onset of spring. The forsythia were abloom in their bright yellows and he noticed the hesitant, first white-pink blossom on a crab apple tree. He inhaled deeply and thought he felt the lump in his throat disappearing. Instinctively he ran his hand over his throat—but of course could feel nothing unusual on the outside.

His driving was like an automatic daze. His mind certainly was not on the road as it should have been. In fact, all driving maneuvers his body did perform were semi-mechanical and from instinctive memory. Waiting at a stop sign, he remembered thinking, *How did I stop the car? Well, I'm glad I did.* He felt his sweaty palms on the steering wheel.

At the intersection, he spotted a young girl walking bouncily ahead in what appeared to be a flowing '60s dress. The pink flowers on the white dress moved nicely with her steps. Every step she took turned her hips just a bit, first to the right, then to the left. The flowing dress translated these movements into happy rotations. As he turned the corner, he noticed that she had blue eyes. His throat throbbed as this stranger mirrored someone from so long ago with whom he now maintained nothing but a lovely, unused, almost forgotten joint memory bank.

Once at home, Ernesto went through the routine of kissing his wife.

"You're early," Primrose noted.

"Yeah, I got hot and now feel the need to take a shower."

"Okay, honey, you got plenty of time 'till dinner. Remember you have church council tonight."

The shower was warm and soothing, but it was the running of the water that seemed to open a flood from within. Ernesto sobbed uncontrollably—he was glad he had locked the door. Once again, he felt his heavy, hot breath struggling past that thick lump in his throat. It sounded like the breathing of an emphysema sufferer.

The recollection of Hanna's power to make him feel whole, swept his body. The thud of his heartbeat, the swelling of the senses recurred as they last did forty years ago when he had wanted to shout for joy and share his ecstasy with the whole world, but the pain of judgment restrained that which was God-given.

He was struck numb by the awareness of the identical feeling after so many years. Again today a feeling of youthful happiness, and again today the need for repression as expected by his status in society, business, and his family. Yet the feeling did not leave. The beauty of innocent first love comes but once. Why had he not been courageous enough long ago to follow instinct rather than society's codes? Codes come and go with the decades, but human instincts only change, if they change, over millions of years. Is it necessary that one must fight the other?

After his shower, he took a walk outside. He stopped by the young magnolia tree he and Primrose had planted a few years earlier. Two solitary, big, healthy, white blossoms graced the small tree. He caressed them both.

It was 2:27 in the morning when he woke up. As he lay there sideways facing his wife he realized that tears were coming from both eyes. The sheet served as a tissue. His wife lay in deep sleep, exhausted from all the many duties she performed so conscientiously as mother, wife, housewife, and professional. She richly deserved the sleep.

Ernesto's mind raced. *Who can I speak with? I need to know what is going on. This pain has got to go away. I have so many responsibilities and opportunities. People depend on me. I can contribute to society in many ways. But this torment is paralyzing me.*

Bursts of despair vented themselves. He used the sheet not only to dry, but also to subdue the sobbing that came from that child-like cry.

He wondered whether she, his beauty of so long ago, was alive. If so, where might she live? Is she happy? Might she ever have had similar feelings? Did his decision back in 1960 cause her the kind of grief he now was experiencing? This may be God's way of punishment. He thought maybe he should see a psychiatrist. His mind skipped about randomly.

He remembered an old country folk custom of whipping a fruit tree. As the tree senses impending disaster, it drives itself toward fruit—its ultimate purpose. And he thought of stories of people on their deathbed, who seem to relate how their life suddenly flashes before them in all its details. Maybe he was soon to die, and God was granting him the view of his beautiful young love as a glimpse of the heavens to come. But then another sweeping thought entered his mind.

A vision of an eternal timeline drew before him. Eons of ages have gone before and eons of ages are likely yet to come. On this endless continuum, two lives have met and miraculously fused into one at a particular time in history. *Is that sheer coincidence? Is it chance without design?* He could not fathom the likelihood.

He thought of the strange tree along the road on the way to work. Two separate roots emerge from the earth becoming two separate trunks, which then join into one trunk several feet above ground. That strong trunk is the source of healthy branches.

Is it my expected duty to continue fighting an honest feeling, subdue what is natural? My life goes on; I am getting older. Is it possible that a seed planted forty years ago suddenly forces a bloom? Should I, can I, follow a natural instinct? How?

The 6:30 a.m. alarm ripped his thoughts back to reality. He had not slept since 2:27 a.m.

3

During the next two weeks the turmoil continued. Nothing really seemed to matter. Ernesto was not interested in the news, in reading, or even in business. He was glad John was so good a chief of staff who now took careful care to run the business extra well. In fact, he gave him virtually unlimited decision-making power—something he would not have done under normal circumstances.

Nothing gave vigor to his being. Four decades ago he had felt that every place, every accomplishment, every house, every profession was utterly empty without her, but could instantly become filled with meaning—if and only if he was with her. He wouldn't have cared where or how they lived, in a small hut in a remote and isolated island village, as long as they lived together. Now again, forty years later he had the exact same feelings. It seemed that no one could offer him enough money, recognition, opportunities or awards—important things up until now—that would have superseded his empty longings. In fact, he became quite calm with the thought of possibly being dismissed by the Board of Directors from his position for incompetence. On one day, he forgot to attend a meeting and just about missed attending and chairing one he had called. He arrived late to that meeting, ashen in face, and went through the business agenda with plastic conviction.

He looked at his calendar for the next several months and wished he could cancel all commitments, all trips, all talks, and all obligations. None were important. Maybe retirement would be the right thing to do now. *I wonder who would like to have all that I have accumulated. I'd like to give it all in exchange for peace of mind.* His thoughts ran in circles.

The crying spells persisted. He wandered the parks of the city hoping to find a cure for the pain of Hanna. Unpredictably while driving, while on the phone, while reading, or even during a meeting, every so often his insides seemed to well up like a massive ocean wave. But it was best to cry in the shower. There it was private, and the warm water seemed to ease the flow.

It was in the basement. There among some other old, long forgotten, and permanently stored things was the envelope. His hand trembled slightly as he lifted it out of the box. Knowing what it contained his throat once again seemed to swell shut; his breath became labored, his palms sweaty, and his mouth dry. Now the visual evidence was once again before him.

More than a dozen old photographs of a young time. Forty years vanished as he saw snapshots of the carefree figure out on a picnic, climbing a tree, or playfully wearing his hat. And there was the formal studio portrait of her in a strapless dress. On the back of one of the pictures she had written, "From your baby," and another said, "From your never forgetting Hanny." *Hanny, that's right,* he thought, that was the affectionate name she liked. He recalled the ecstasy of getting her letters. He instantly recognized them by the handwriting, the blue ballpoint lettering on the return address that spelled magic: H.V.

But most of all he was overtaken by the intimacy of the studio portraits of the two of them. These black and white pieces of art had just the right shadings and contrasts in light for perfect balance. Their heads were tilted lovingly toward each other; their eyes wide open with innocence and expectation. He recalled the pride the studio obviously took in the portrait when it chose to display it in the window for months to come. He remembered his anxiety at seeing the display: what if his friends or parents discover it; will they sneer, criticize, or preach? But mostly he remembered his pride: the rest of the world also recognized that which he had discovered, a boundless beauty. Ernesto and Hanna were obviously made for one another.

All the beauty of first love now returned to him in bubbling abundance. He beheld her with total purity of thought, and in this mirror of the mind she was reflected spotlessly. He did not want to let go of the feeling. And to his pleasant dismay, the pictures still did not evoke sexual arousal, but rather a feeling of preserving white innocence and intimate friendship. Soon, however, a new feeling did creep in.

He became jealous. Jealous of those who had seen her all these years, those who saw her now this very instant, jealous of lost time, jealous of those who were now infected by her cheerfulness and vigor, her zest for life, her playfulness; jealous of anything that comes close to her, her neighbors, friends, coworkers, even a husband? He could not comprehend that someone else would be allowed to be with her, have her. A deep emptiness wished to be filled by holding her close. Was it the impossibility to possess her that made that wish so attractive? He considered whether he was jealous of her husband? Well, was she even married? he wondered. He had no information, but was certain that she had married—such a beautiful rose would not be left unpicked. Was he jealous of her husband, whoever he was? That was preposterous! She had to live her life, choose her husband. She could not be expected to let life go by while everyone else went on. Maybe she was the same unchanged girl, waiting. No, she did deserve a husband, sexual satisfaction, a family—of course she did!

But he did wonder. Did she, during the time of laughing courtship with another, did she ever recall a first love, long ago in a far away world? Was he her first love?

Might she, during the dancing delirium of her wedding feast, might she have thought about him but once?

Was it possible that perhaps in the midst of the steaming, wild passion of her never-ending honeymoon nights culminating in the heat of intimate encounters, was it possible that she might have spent one single fleeting moment on remembrance of someone else, of good times now gone, of long ago molded hopes now faded, of an anticipated perfect union now being chained to another?

And in all the succeeding years, during her husband's many advances, often attacks, in which he possessed her with a male-dominated demand of ownership and right, and to which she yielded ever more out of duty than out of joy—and more and more so as time went on—did she, during these one-sided pleasure plunders lay there and think of her past, once so promising and glorious? When his two-minute escapades, which usually resulted in his immediate and deep sleep, when these escapades were not enough time to awaken within her the needed desire, did she wonder and wish for someone who would be kind and gentle during the day, who would help her with the daily chores, who would join her in taking care of the children, who would do the dishes, who would give her an occasional day off, and who would give her repeated loving embraces? Did she imagine that sweating face dripping about her, that ever-fatter body of his spilling over hers, did she then close her eyes and imagine another face and another trim body of someone else she had known in the tropics—of someone she had loved, had wanted, had dreamed about, and had desired to be consumed and completed with and made one with?

Ernesto did wonder: was he jealous?

Ernesto would look at the pictures a lot during the ensuing days. Again he found himself caught between contemporary morals and God-given drives. Why did this happen to him? After all, he had in life all he could possibly want. He was professionally accomplished, had reached the top of the success ladder higher and faster than he had ever expected, was financially secure, had a complete and intact family, had not suffered setbacks, disappointments, or pain, had done extensive, worldwide travel, enjoyed prestige, was sought out and sought after, gifted and talented, had matured intellectually, socially, and spiritually. Why then these feelings of remorse, of what ifs? Maybe it was because he had turned sixty and was facing a midlife crisis; maybe he was tired of basing all of life's decisions on the power of the intellect. Maybe cerebral success is not fundamental to life. He saw more and more truth in the little quote he had broken from a Chinese fortune cookie: "The heart is wiser than the intellect." All his life he had worked with achieving, success-driven women. Maybe he missed interaction with women who took time to be women. Perhaps man eventually reverts to that which is most basic and precious in life. Maybe the need for ultimate internal beauty wins out in the end. But why then must there be pain with beauty? Is it possible that the most beautiful in this world is reserved for that which is most painful? Can beauty emerge only through pain?

He recalled that on one of his trips south to visit his parents he had briefly met a lady after a church service, younger than him, who confided in him that she still remembered his beautiful courtship with Hanna. The lady said that she was a young and impressionable girl at the time, but very observant. She talked to other girls her age about it and they all agreed: that is a nice pair. She said that to her, the Ernesto and Hanna union was a good example of what she hoped she might one day emulate. Then she asked:

"Did you ever get married to her?"

"No." That was not easy to say.

"Well, I wanted to let you know that you were a good example to many." Then she disappeared into the crowd.

Ernesto stood there mouthing the words: "Thank you."

That night, Ernesto dreamed he had brought Hanna home to the Bauman family of long ago in the far away country of the *conquistadores*. Life at home was normal and her impending addition to the family somehow was very much expected. He loved her, loved her much; she was his natural mate, his other self. He belonged to her and she to him. She was included by all—even by Father. He introduced her to what had earlier been critics. They now welcomed her. Ernesto's joy soared to the highest heavens. He strove to earn her praise by accomplishing great things. He walked about straight and erect, aware of his health and proud to be with her. He was made whole by his glorious Hanna. Ernesto did not want the dream to end.

He made a compulsive decision to call his father and confront him with the unresolved issue of long ago, buried for so long in the clouds of forgetting, but now revived with lightening clarity.

"How are you? How are the kids? How is Primrose?"

"They are fine, and how are you both?"

"Well, you know we are doing fine considering our age."

The conversation began in the normal manner and would have taken the expected direction of inquiry regarding health, and work, and community, and domestic details. However, Ernesto took the bold step never before taken.

"Dad, I want to talk to you about something from forty years ago, when I was still at home." His throat dried and his hands became moist.

Silence. Then a hesitant

"Yes?"

"Dad, I want to talk to you about the girlfriend I had. Do you remember Hanna?"

"Yes?"

"Well, I have not thought about her but very fleetingly during the last forty years. I have no idea where she is, if she is alive, or what she does but a few months ago, I had an earthquake-like recollection of feeling about her—about our love and feelings of remorse over things gone wrong. The turmoil persists and won't leave me."

146

He paused, giving a chance for response, which did not come.

"I want you to know, I have a good wife, and our relationship is sound and healthy, and this upheaval is not the result in any kind of marital difficulties. But I want you to know that I carry some animosity toward you for not accepting my girl forty years ago. You spoke and interacted with the girls of my friends, but you never once spoke to my girl. You spoke to my friends about their girls and gave hints of approval, but to me you spoke but once and that was in a derogatory way about her. What, may I ask, was wrong with her?"

Silence.

"Dad, I want to know. I need to know. What was wrong with her?"

"Ernesto, this is hard and it is such old agenda."

"Dad, I am struggling for my sanity. You have to tell me."

"Well, she did not have a good reputation."

"How in the world can you say such a thing? How could you make such a judgment, when you never even spoke to her? Did you ask others about her? Did you show any interest in finding out? She was your son's girlfriend, remember?"

"Well, I don't know, son."

"Dad, I am going to find out if she is alive, and if she is, I am going to contact her."

"Ernesto, I would suggest..."

"Dad, I do not want your suggestions. You know a love affair is a matter between two people and two people only. No one else knows what is being built and no one has the right to interfere. That is not the way God has ordained mankind to function.

"Dad, would you do me a favor?"

"I'll try."

"I want you to write a letter to her addressing your position toward her forty years ago. I would like for you to address her in the polite form, and I would like to have you send the letter to me so I can read it, so that when I do find her I can share it with her. You see, Dad, I am wounded in a way that is most surprising to me, but I am wounded deeply, and I am searching for a cure. My life is not at peace. I have a wonderful wife who makes me proud, she is a superb mother to our children, and she is an accomplished professional. Nevertheless, had your disposition toward my girl been different that long time ago, my life would have taken a different direction. Maybe that would not have been for the good, but right now I hurt deeply. Will you write?"

"I will."

"Dad, I love you."

His registered letter came within the week.

4

It became hard for Ernesto to conceal his anguish. He had, apparently, convinced his family that he was tired. They suggested that it might be time for a vacation to unwind. He did think they were entitled to an explanation. Primrose, though, was far more insightful. She had read the anguish on his face, noticed his dazed look, his lack of appetite, and his slow loss of weight, which on his trim physique became quite noticeable.

"What is working on you, honey? You look so pale and drawn. Are things not going right at the office?"

He was able to postpone a discussion for several days and Primrose waited patiently. In his briefcase that day, he found a note: "I love you, Primrose." Usually she did not share so overtly, and it touched him.

At the thought of perhaps being destined to a life of silent agony, he used the powers of his so carefully groomed self-discipline and determined to take action. The simple act of so deciding relit his fighting spirit and he indeed was ready to move. The burst of vitality raised its head and threw back its shoulders in upright position—an accustomed position indicating he was in control. At first, he considered engaging the services of a private detective agency, but then decided to make a move, which allowed him tight control. He called Jane to summon his chief of staff.

John entered with a gesture of resolute hope that things were back to normal.

"John, I want you to do some detective research."

"Say again, you want me to do what?" he questioned.

"I want you to find a person on whom I have very little."

John thought he saw the meaning. "You're into a deal with a questionable character?"

"No, no, not so. I would like for you to find a person whose maiden name some forty years ago was Hanna Voran. She moved from South America to Winnipeg in early 1959 with her widowed mother, a sister, and two brothers. If she is alive, I suspect she is married and carries a different name. Find her. Get me a profile.

Research her life. Find out as much as you can: her whereabouts, her date of birth, marital status, children, what is important to her, medical history, employment, education, church life, her friends, what convictions does she have, what makes her tick, what is her husband like, how is her married life, how does she relate to her family. Oh, and John, get me pictures if you can."

"Whoa!" was his only response.

John left with the most puzzled look of his life, wisely avoiding the nagging question on his mind. Ernesto was certain he would do his duty well.

Ernesto suddenly had the urge to share his feelings—even with just a piece of paper. At a loss of who to turn to he resorted to a means he had used successfully all his professional life. He distilled the essence of the issue and committed it to paper.

In 1958/60 I had an intensely romantic (non-sexual) relationship with a beautiful young lady—our lives fused into one. Her family moved to Canada and we kept corresponding.

Distance and time cooled the relationship. I married someone else (am still married to the same good person), have a nice family, and a good profession. During all these years, I have never again seen her, written to, spoken with, or heard of or from my first love. Occasionally I might have thought of her in passing.

A few months ago (some forty years after), I suddenly experienced an emotional volcano and my thoughts now return to her constantly. Where has life taken her? Is she alive? Could I visit with her? I find tears erupting spontaneously day or night and I do not know what is happening.

It felt good to write.

Ernesto's days were restless, his nights sleepless. He found himself daydreaming, studying a map of Winnipeg, wondering if she saw the same moon he saw, wondering what she did. Flashes of anger surfaced, which centered on the agony of having saved the purity of a girl, only to allow someone else to have her. Was this how one would feel upon giving a daughter in marriage?

Primrose had gently encouraged him to share his burden—whatever it was. They went to bed early that night, turned out the light, and she held his hand—and waited. Slowly he began to talk and soon he talked as he had seldom done. He shared of his explosion of sudden feelings, his torment, his utter frustration, his confusion as to what it all meant, his nagging desire to know about his first love. The talking relieved his feelings and Primrose was the perfect counselor who listened patiently and spoke soothing words. It took two hours before the flood of feeling was poured out. Relieved, they embraced. He was so proud of his wife's strength and her steadfastness.

Primrose lay there wondering about the meaning of this. Was her husband overworked, was he stretched too thin? What would be the consequences of his feelings? What was he thinking, planning?

"You ought to go see her," she said gently, but got no response.

Ernesto lay there in awe of his feeling of closeness to his wife. Was this a way of renewing the deepness of a relationship perhaps somewhat tarnished by time and familiarity. He held her closely as though hoping for... he did not know what.

He was scheduled to leave for Chicago on business. Never before had he felt so resistant to travel. Instead, he came to Primrose every few minutes for an embrace and a gentle kiss on her cheek. He kept postponing the trip again and again, holding her hand, putting his head on her neck, and wanting to be close. Eventually he did go—and Primrose went to the library to check out a book on male middle-age crisis, materials she eventually shared with her confused spouse.

In Chicago, Ernesto found some relief in continuing the journaling about his feelings. In fact, he found that doing so was quite therapeutic and about the only escape from the sordid pain. He wrote early in the morning, at lunch time, between meetings, even during meetings and again late at night. During those four days of meetings not once did he buy a paper or turn on the TV. He ate minimally, but walked the streets endlessly and without aim. His eyes searched the crowds for women in their late fifties. How did they look, behave, walk, and talk? He hoped that his first love would now be old, wrinkled, heavy, and unkempt. He thought that might relieve the urge to see her. But then he realized the urge was not based on physical attraction but on a deep felt need to jointly dip into an old and beautiful memory pool belonging only to the two of them. All of his activities and thoughts were considered in light of his remembrances of long ago.

It did occur to him that perhaps this was all a symptom of an internal body change. Perhaps a sudden rush of blood had flushed old brain cells, as through a stroke, thereby awakening those long forgotten images and feelings. In fact, he thought that his heartbeat was perhaps arrhythmic. A courtesy blood pressure check in the lobby of the hotel produced a wide-eyed nurse's strong urging to take a quiet walk, have beautiful thoughts, and return a bit later. The unchanged results sent her scurrying for a doctor, and a medical check-up later revealed very high blood pressure.

5

Coincidences have a way of popping up unexpectedly. They bring together, often in most unusual ways, events and circumstances apparently unrelated to each other. They appear at most surprising times and are, at times, unbelievable. So it was with this one.

Some time in the past Ernesto had corresponded with an author on the west coast who had written an interesting book. The reason he contacted her was not the book, though that was the pretense, the reason was that she, too, had migrated from the south, had established herself in the U.S., and had become a successful author. During the communication with her, Ernesto had mentioned that at one point he had dated a girl whom she might know; her name was Hanna Voran.

"Did you know Hanna?"

"Yes, I did, and still do."

The emphasis on the "still do" was mildly surprising, but he did not pursue it, and the conversation ended there.

While away on business on the east coast he received a late night call from this author on the west coast. How she got a hold of him he never learned, but the obvious amount of work involved in tracking him down indicated the importance of the matter.

"I would like to talk about Hanna." The minute Hanna's name came up, his interest piqued and he wondered what else might come.

"You see, in our home country I had a boyfriend and we were happily floating on the bliss of our youth, allowing it to move us into the future." She spoke in refined language.

"But then I found out that my boyfriend had been seeing Hanna, your Hanna." She was silent for a bit waiting for a reaction, which did not come. Ernesto could not believe it. He thought at first that Hanna having a relationship with someone else might be natural. It must have been before she knew him. But why had she never told him about it? Why did she always avoid talking about the past, her past, her settlement? While it was a surprise, it would be acceptable.

"There is more that I want to tell you." Her announcement came almost like a warning. What would she reveal now?

"They saw each other while he also saw me." It almost stopped his heart from pumping.

"There is more."

Ernesto could not fathom there being more information and almost said that he was not interested. But being too stunned to talk, the voice from the west continued.

"Hanna and my boyfriend had an intimate relationship."

Silence.

"When I found out, I was furious. We fought loudly and extensively; we nearly broke up, but eventually we worked it out and we stayed together—for a while. Our marriage did eventually break up." Her confident voice revealed truth.

Ernesto was not interested in her part of the story, but instead, his mind went into high-fever gear.

"You know, Hanna was just fifteen at the time. My boyfriend was twenty-two. He was tall, dark, handsome, rode his horse in a stately manner so as to sweep all the girls off their feet. I guess it is understandable."

She seemed to excuse her. Ernesto could not. He was anxious to hang up.

He processed for weeks. Why would she do such a thing? Why did she never tell him? Perhaps she was too young, a mere child of fifteen. What if she had begotten a new life; he may have never known her. She would be abandoned in the settlement. Would he still take the joy she had brought him, in exchange for the truth that she was something other than he knew her to be? After much time had passed, he would eventually be able to say "yes."

This explained so many other things in their past relationship. For instance, whenever he had asked, "Do you love me?" she would never answer directly. She would change the subject, answer in what he had thought were clever ways of saying "Yes." He recalled that she would at times tell him that she has no right to express her feelings. He had thought that was perhaps a way of saying that she did not want to, or perhaps that she could not, or perhaps, heaven forbid, that she did not have such feelings.

He could understand that, Marta, Hanna's mother had also had a stormy relationship with Peter, and it was not to the liking of her father. But eventually they got married. So, her mother had an affair, and perhaps Hanna's affair could be excused?

Is that what Ernesto's father had always meant when he talked about being careful what company you are in, or about Hanna not having a good name or a good reputation? Why did his father never tell him? Did others know also? No one had ever told him.

He recalled her quiet smiles, sometimes discreet, concealing rather than revealing whatever went on in her mind; he remembered her flirting with young fellows. Was she just young, carefree, and enjoying life, or was she loose?

Ernesto felt betrayed and trapped. Perhaps all his feelings were just puppy love for someone, while younger, apparently so much more experienced. He felt taken advantage of by a young girl who had lived life to the fullest with one, and then looked to exploit life with another—or perhaps even with both. Was she a slut after all? No, that could not be. The writer from the west must be wrong, or perhaps not telling the truth.

On the other hand, he could understand how impressionable she might have been. She had beaten all the other girls vying for attention from this handsome cowboy riding high down the street on his stately horse, a village-recognized symbol of superiority.

Ernesto sank into a deep pit of loneliness and despair; the extrovert Ernesto withdrew into himself, becoming an introvert. He liked the idea of becoming a hermit, cocooning into himself, not going out, not eating much, absorbing the silence around him. He isolated himself from people, from colleagues, from family. He even isolated himself from his wife: he became solitary—socially, emotionally, and physically withdrawn.

As the days, weeks, and months passed, he processed the events from all possible angles almost to the exclusion of everything else. His job suffered, his family suffered, his health suffered. He was particularly concerned about his job where colleagues mostly left him alone, and staff, whom he worked with closely, noticed his turmoil and made occasional inquiries. In his vulnerability, like that of a drunken man, he occasionally threw himself recklessly at their mercy, exposing more than he wanted. His doctor treated him for very high blood pressure.

Time did pass—but, contrary to its legendary power, it proved to be no healer. He sought refuge in music by listening to Mozart's *Requiem* and *Misa Solemnis,* to Beethoven's *Emperor, Ninth Symphony,* and the *Piano Concertos.*

He sought solace in films such as *Casablanca, An Officer and a Gentleman, Dr. Zhivzgo, Rebecca, Babette's Feast, The African Queen, The Accidental Tourist, The Mission, Chariots of Fire, My Brother's Wife;* and in plays such as *Love Letters.*

But mostly he immersed himself in readings where he looked for help: Ethel Spector Person, *Dreams of Love* and *Fateful Encounters;* Boris Pasternak, *Dr. Zhivago;* Lesly Blanch, *The Wilder Shores of Love;* Harold Brodkey, *First Love and Other Sorrows;* Daphne DuMaurier, *Jamaica Inn* and *Rebecca;* Ivan Turgenev, *Spring Torrents,* and *Assya;* Fred H. Steward, *Six Weeks;* Inga Dean, *Memory and Desire;* Gwen Bristow, *This Side of Glory,* and *Tomorrow is Forever;* Harold Bell Wright, *Shepherd of the Hills;* Johann W. von Goethe, *The Sorrows of the Young Werther;* Erich Fromm, *The Art of Loving;* Gabriel Garcia Marquez, *One Hundred Years of Solitude* and *Love in the Time of Cholera;* Danielle Steel, *To Love Again;* Judith Krantz, *Mistral's Daughter;* Jeanne Stephens, *Mexican Nights;* Juan Valera, *Pepita Jiménez;* and many others.

And eventually a more mature and level-headed attitude surfaced—and in the end won out. What the heck! She was just a child, was not yet a church member, and was entitled to sow a few wild oats. After all, today such a thing is not that uncommon. These events happened long ago to a very young girl who had no father, no education, had been torn from her stable Russian society at a very young age, had traveled the ocean for a long seven weeks on a mismanaged and wrecked ship, and learned to live solely by her instincts. Since then, forty years had passed. Yet, the fact remained that his first love was Hanna, whether or not he was *her* first love. He resolved to seek the higher ground and approach the matter from a mature point of view. He made up his mind to let her past be bygone.

John had been working diligently on the assigned task of finding someone named Hanna, who moved to Canada in 1959. To no one's surprise, John had done his research well. He handed his boss a crisp, clean folder. Ernesto was curious how he might have gotten all the information, but he was now much too interested in the contents rather than the process. Ernesto received the folder, briefly glanced inside, and saw at least two pages of information. He quickly decided to leave the office and start driving to some quiet place where he parked the car and carefully started reading.

Name:
- Hanna Voran Bender
- (phone and address were listed)

Husband:
- Josh Bender, factory worker, deceased

Married:
- July 1963, three children
- lost first child to heart defect

Details:
- works as room attendant at the Enterprise Hotel
- mother and sister passed away
- brothers still live nearby
- has never returned to the country of her youth
- does not like to travel
- appears to be happy
- shows many visits to the doctor
- apparent chronic illness
- medical records unobtainable

Relieved, Ernesto returned to the office and immediately called the magic number in Winnipeg. He was surprised to find that the number had quickly become emblazoned in his mind. He let it ring only once—just to convince himself that such a phone did exist. Maybe at another time, he would let it ring longer. "I wonder why the many visits to the doctor," he muttered.

Immediately he had to leave on a three-hour trip to give a series of talks. Without ever stopping the car, without any music or other distractions, he allowed his mind to wander and wonder. Late that evening he returned, again allowing his thoughts to go where they may.

Early the next morning he called John to his office.

"Did we ever get any invitations from Winnipeg for my talks and workshops?" he asked.

"Yeah, I think we do occasionally. But you know the policy that you yourself set long ago: Go only where the big crowd is for the big payoff. So I never scheduled you for Winnipeg."

"Go check the latest invitations from Winnipeg and see if we can appear there next week. Let them do heavy and quick advertising. We'll pay the extra expense."

John protested. "I don't want to argue with you, but that will be a waste of time—a money-losing venture. We'll probably draw only about a hundred people at most."

"All the same, John, I want to give my standard talk to the Winnipeg business community. Oh, and have us stay at the Enterprise Hotel, and let's have the meeting there as well."

"With all due respect, that won't work."

"Why not?" Ernesto demanded.

"Because the Enterprise is not our kind of hotel. We wouldn't want to book it for our event. Besides, they have an assembly room that holds barely fifty people."

"Book the Enterprise," Ernesto said firmly, "and have them move some walls or do something to make the assembly room larger."

"For next week?"

"Friday of next week at the latest!"

John scratched his head and went to work.

6

The plane ride to Winnipeg was routine and uneventful. Ernesto sat by the window, John and the others sat away at a distance. He stared into the vastness below and as time went by, he sensed the land below becoming special—it beheld his first love.

Ernesto felt pulled toward her with an uncontrollable power as that of an ocean under toe. He had an inner urge to hold Hanna's hand, to talk with her, to reminisce, to shed a tear. This feeling would have been the same if she were old and wrinkled, poor and abandoned, fat and unkempt, rich and famous, or the lighthearted girl he knew forty years ago. He felt no sexual attraction, but only friendship now rekindled mightily.

He regretted that he had not had the courage of his feelings back in 1960. Had he only been risky, bold, standing up to his parents rather than being a parent pleaser! Instead of following society's expectations, he wished he would have followed God's so obvious leading in his heart and gotten married to his sweetheart, come what may. For all of this he wanted to apologize to Hanna.

Suddenly he felt embarrassed of the very thoughts he harbored. Still he wondered how things might have turned out. He thought of his friends who led double lives and fear suddenly gripped his throat dangerously.

He wondered about her double life? Did she feel guilty about it? Certainly, she must have! Did she still lead a double life? Certainly not!

"What would you like for dinner? We have a choice of chicken or steak..." a smiling flight attendant offered. While others around him ate and drank, he refused all intake, instead studying the flat landscape below.

His thoughts now turned to his own approach to life in the last forty years. Was it possible, he thought, that the powerful, driving force for success so dominant within him was a subconscious attempt of his innermost being to attain that which he could not? At first that force may have been channeled to please those who placed expectations on him. Receiving little praise, did the drive then

159

unknowingly transform into a desperate attempt to reach and hold that which was out of reach? He wondered if perhaps this was a way in which he strove to conquer yet another, higher challenge—the ultimate, the impossible challenge. He found no answers, but one thing became clear in his mind. Intellectual powers can conquer and dominate things, ideas, money, power, and people, but they cannot fulfill the innermost desires of the heart. The mind can busy itself, even ignore the needs of the heart, but it cannot fulfill the longings of a thirsty soul.

He thought of the interview he had recently heard where a psychologist had explained the phenomenon of sudden recall. It is possible, so the psychologist said, that a traumatic experience with powerful emotional impact can be wiped out of the conscious and hurled deep into the subconscious, there to lie dormant for years or decades overshadowed by the trivial and mundane. It is a self-defense mechanism developed by the psyche to protect itself from potential huge damage. But the emotion is not dead, it is only dormant and often will, given the right catalyst, explode into the conscious, overshadowing all else and forcefully demanding its due healing—now.

They checked into the best rooms of the Enterprise. His first action was to call Housekeeping. He was afraid to, but eventually picked up the receiver.

"Is Mrs. Bender there?" He felt timid as a schoolboy calling the principal's office.

"Mrs. Bender, who's calling, please?" it was a scratchy male voice seemingly being used against its own will.

"A friend."

"Well, if she's here, she's supposed to work."

"I know, all I need to know is if she's in, please."

"Let me see, she's supposed to come by four, so she should be here by now, but she's been out so much lately, and I know she called in sick yesterday; so let me go check the board."

The gruffy voice disappeared for a long time, and then eventually returned. "Yeah, she checked in. But during work hours she ain't supposed to talk to nobody on the phone or in person."

"Okay, thank you."

160

Hanna thought there were a lot of people in the building tonight. Someone said there was supposed to be some meeting. They had even torn up some walls to make room for more seats. She thought of all the cleanup work this would mean for tomorrow.

As she dusted the coffee tables in the lounge, her eyes caught a book the gentleman sitting nearby had just laid down. Her first glance was superfluous, but something urged her to return the glance: *The Source of Success*. But her eyes were drawn to the lower portion of the book where the author's name was: by Ernesto Bauman. Momentarily forgetting her role, she sat down by the table and picked up the book, held it, and rechecked the name. One hand was absent-mindedly dusting the same spot on the table over and over again. Could this be a coincidence? Her pulse beat faster. She turned to the back cover and there was the picture of the familiar, now older, more mature, perhaps more distinguished face.

She felt a glance from the gentleman who had laid the book down. Suddenly feeling embarrassed at her boldness, she quickly put the book down, but he smiled and motioned for her to continue. She fanned the pages several times, stopped here and there, really not reading—just staring. She closed the book, held it firmly, and studied the picture.

Long dormant remembrances surfaced as she held the book. She thought about her youth, her arrival in the big city as a teenager, and the joy of love. She remembered the carefree times in the tropics, and all the goodness life seemed to offer. They had had so many unspoken hopes and dreams. She once again felt the pain of separation, the letters, and the distancing of the affair. She relived the endless time of wondering, waiting, hoping, maybe... She wished she would have taken him up to go see him in college, in spite of... She remembered the studio portrait of the two of them which she had blown up and redone in color. It had hung in her room for a long time, where she admired the intense brown eyes of her love. But eventually, as the distant cooling winds blew, it made its way into a trunk where it still rested to this day. She had often thought about him, especially every year on his birthday. At opportune moments, she had inquired as to his whereabouts.

She thought of her new love affair to which she gave herself with hopeful, yet exhausted energy, her marriage, her work, the parties she gave, the lonely fishing station where she liked to sit and daydream the impossible dream. She thought of her children and the time she had spent urging them to get a good education to the extent of offering to pay all their expenses as long as they stayed in school. She thought of her ailment and the energy it now sapped from her life.

But then she again looked at the picture on the back of the book and it seemed she was flushed with the energy of a second youth. Something seemed to relight in her heart the cold and forgotten ashes of the passion of her youth.

"Excuse me, sir, what do you know about this book?" She once again surprised herself with her own boldness as she spoke to the stranger in the other seat.

The gentleman looked at her, seeming to see a different woman than he had seen just a few minutes before. There was a personal charm about her, a tenderness of femininity that was being reflected in a certain restored passion in her eyes.

"Oh, you don't know him? He's Dr. Ernesto Bauman, a businessman and educator from the U.S. He's here to give a talk tonight."

Could it be? Could it be? She quickly went back to work. Her happy face mirrored beautiful thoughts while her hands moved mechanically performing chores so well memorized over the years.

7

Ernesto was restless. Pacing up and down in his room, he had been reviewing his notes for the talk. There really was no need to do so, since he knew the talk well, had given it many, many times, and felt completely at ease with the subject of his experience. Still, he preferred to lay out the notes in front of him during the talk to remind him of the special emphasis he planned to make here and there. After all, his father had always told him that if the knees don't jerk just a bit before a speech, something is wrong. He inserted the examples of local Winnipeg success stories, which his staff had researched and written up for him. This was a technique he had used so well in all his speeches. It gave the audience proof that this guy was serious about what he was doing and it provided a sense of "I can," of personal ownership in what was being said.

Ernesto glanced at the clock: it was 5:05 pm, nearly two and a half hours to the start of the meeting. On an impulse, he called John to join him on a walk down to the hotel meeting room to get a feel for the lay of the land and to talk about the plans for the evening. As they walked down the hall discussing examples of local successes, they did not, at first, notice the woman in front of them pushing a room attendant's cart in the same direction but about thirty feet ahead of them. When she heard their voices she stopped, frozen, and waited, her hands firmly clasping the handle of the cart.

Suddenly, Ernesto, too, stopped and fixed his eyes on the back profile of the woman now only about ten feet in front of him. He immediately recognized her. He felt that familiar thread of icy sweat running down his back. He studied her appearance from head to toe noting with pleasure that she stood as erect and proud as ever; her shoulders were laid back, her chin up. Her once girlish figure had filled and developed in a way becoming of her age, giving her feminine charms an aura of maturity. Her hair was done simply and the occasional graying streaks seemed to belong.

John broke the silence. "Ernesto, are you coming? We don't have all the time in the world."

"John, you go ahead, I'll come later," he instructed.

163

"What am I supposed to do, tell the others that you're standing out in the hall?"

"John, just go and check out the room, then go on upstairs."

Rolling his eyes, John went. The hall was now empty except for two people who had not looked at each other in forty years.

Ernesto stepped forward a few more paces.

"I'll see you in the morning," Ernesto said quietly. He thought his own voice sounded strange.

Ernesto moved ahead slowly until he came up to her, then he leaned against the wall opposite from where she was standing. Hanna had not moved, but he could now see her left profile well. Then she slowly moved her head toward him, and once again Ernesto found himself face to face with his first angel's blue eyes. They stood there in silent awe of the event, with their eyes fixed on each other. They felt their blood tumbling violently through their veins and their hearts beating noisily against their chests. A long history flashed through their minds bringing onto the stage of recall a young love, a lost love, a deep sorrow, a trail of tears; but the replay seemed to come to rest on the happiness of those days long, long ago in a country far, far away.

Ernesto moved up to the cart and slowly put his right hand onto her left hand with its knuckles white from the still firm grip clutching the cart handle. It took every bit of self-control to hide the lump in his throat that seemed on the verge of strangling him. They looked at each other in silence, a silence they were afraid to interrupt, yet were embarrassed to continue. And then it happened, that gentle embrace caused by a force unknown to either, which neither initiated, yet both expected. The embrace was short but he continued to hold her upper arms.

"Hanna, how are you?"

"I'm fine, how are you?" Their quivering voices betrayed the deep emotion.

"Do you have any idea how glad I am to see you?" he asked.

"I'm so surprised to see you here! What are you doing here?"

"Hanna, can we talk somewhere?"

With a shy smile, she motioned ahead to a side door. She pushed the cart just up to the door where she left it, then entered. It was a supply closet, but it did have a small table and two chairs. A single

164

bare lamp hung from the ceiling. She leaned the mop against the wash basin and then they sat down across from each other. He took her clasped hands into his and gazed into her face. The lines revealed maturity, her eyes, as blue as ever, still held what now was a rekindled youthful fire, but which seemed unable to hide a distant sadness. The left side of her lower lip still had that little dimple that identified her as Hanna. Neither knew what to say.

"Where do we begin?" was Hanna's attempt, but Ernesto spoke at the same time:

"Tell me about yourself. Tell me about yourself, your family, your children," he repeated.

"I have three kids… but how did you know I had a family?"

"I did some checking."

"Are you married? Do you have a family? Where do you live? What is your work? What hobbies do you have? Who is your wife? Are you happy? How did you find me? What do you want here?" Her questions spilled as from a broken dam.

They exchanged information about their families, their brothers and sisters, their parents, work, and other such safe topics. They spoke of their hobbies, their spouses, their favorite activities, their good times and hard times.

"Did you ever get your electronics degree you wanted?" she inquired.

"No, I did go in a different direction, education and business."

"I did know you were married to a teacher, I asked some people. All these years I always think about you on your birthday."

Long silence. He was astonished.

Then, like with the flip of a switch, she brought them back to reality: "But what are you doing here?"

"During the last months I suddenly have been tormented a lot and am now constantly thinking about you and us long ago and the good times we had. I have been wondering about you and your life," Ernesto confessed.

"We did have an intense, beautiful, innocent, and very good relationship, didn't we?" Ernesto was pleased to no end to hear her say that.

"I am so glad I found you. Tell me, can you still run as fast as you did?"

"I am no longer the same person you knew four decades ago."

Silence.

"Hanna, tell me about you. Whatever happened between us? Are you happy?"

Before she could answer, a loud knock followed by an immediate opening of the door interrupted the private communion. There by the door stood the body of the supervisor that carried that gruff voice Ernesto remembered from the telephone: "Hanna, you're not on break, are you?"

Ernesto immediately rose, walked out, and put his arm on the supervisor's shoulder, moving into the hall. He pulled out a large bill, gave it to the startled supervisor, and asked, "Do you suppose you can find someone else so she can have the rest of the evening off? Oh, and do keep Hanna on the payroll for tonight, please." A hesitant, somewhat embarrassed smile crossed the supervisor's face. Then he took the money and left.

Ernesto returned to the small table where Hanna still sat, transfixed.

"They gave you time off for the rest of the evening."

Both sat in silence looking at each other. Far from their youth, now in the summer of their years, they were two mature people who shared a deep common memory bank of a past that belonged to two who no longer were. He noticed a tear running down her cheek. With the back of his index finger, he wiped it gently, as he had done so long ago.

"What is it, Hanna?"

"I'm mad with joy."

Suddenly, they both felt liberated to talk freely.

From her purse, she produced a small black-and-white passport-sized photograph of herself, obviously taken in her teenage years.

"Do you know what this is?" she asked.

"Well, it is a picture of you, and I would like a copy."

"I always keep it in my purse because it is the picture I had taken in 1960 in preparation for the documents to come to the U.S. to see you."

"Oh my God! So, why did you not come? Do you have any idea how much I was yearning to see you then? I was so lonely. My life revolved around you."

"Well, remember at the time you wrote me a letter saying that for Thanksgiving you were going to visit a friend in Nebraska."

"Yes, I remember, I went with my roommate to his home."

"Your roommate? Oh my God! I thought you had a girlfriend in Nebraska. Isn't your wife from Nebraska?"

"No."

Again, there was a long silence, eventually broken by her shaking sigh. "Oh, my God, my God! You mean I decided not to come to the U.S. because I thought you... Oh my God! You mean our possible future was determined by a misunderstanding? Oh, my God! Oh, my God!"

"Hanna, would you have married me?"

"Of course I would have."

Both were lost in their thoughts of what ifs.

"You know, Hanna, my parents were against it. I was struggling to study, had no money, was trying to get used to the new environment, kept thinking about the opinion of people back home—you remember they were against this—I was confused, utterly confused. Did you suffer as much then as I suffer now?"

She answered not.

"I am sorry," was the only thing he could say.

"Will you come with me to the auditorium? I have to give a speech."

She seemed pleased.

The crowd had gathered down below in the makeshift auditorium, ready to be inspired by the talk on "The Sources of Success." Given the short public notice for this meeting, many had hastily rearranged their schedules to be here. Some already had Bauman's book on the topic, had brought it along to continue reading, or have it autographed or both. The happy chatter spoke of the air of expectancy that permeated the crowd. Everyone was here to see and hear Ernesto Bauman.

They reached the stage door where they were met by several assistants. Inside, Ernesto could hear John talking to the audience about his boss's company, success, and books. Through the short delay everyone was now worked up to heightened expectation. As the side door opened the crowd got a glimpse of Ernesto and rose to its feet in applause. Ernesto led Hanna to the front row. An assistant prepared an extra seat at front row center. Before she sat down, they shared a bonding smile. Then Ernesto went to the podium.

The crowd still stood in applause, but his eyes were fixed on Hanna there radiantly absorbing the happening. As usual, the speech had been neatly laid out in front of him. He knew all the nuances, the pauses, the plunges for emphases, the one-liners. It was a speech fine-tuned over the years with scientific precision: 50% content, 45% stories, 5% jokes. The jokes appeared every seven to nine minutes and lasted no more than 22 seconds each. The entire speech was exactly 55 minutes.

The crowd had settled by now. He looked at Hanna and instinctively made a bold decision. He closed the speech notes, put them on the shelf below, and with his eyes fixed on the center front row, he began to speak from the heart.

"Ladies and gentleman, fellow travelers on this Earth.

"You have come tonight to hear about the sources of success. As you may know, I have given speeches on the topic many times before and have written about it. In fact, some of you may have read my book. In it, I have laid out the many components of success as I saw them at the time. They are all based on cold analytical reasoning, dissection of facts, shrewdness of approach, and decisiveness of action. The book emphasizes a five step approach: Kindle that inner fire of drive; educate yourself through preparation of the intellect, feelings, body, and soul; make a detailed plan; surround yourself with good people; work the plan judiciously. You can read about it in the book. But, I just made a decision to depart from the standard approach. Allow me to share my thoughts on a deeper subject, namely that of true friendship.

"We live life but once. We are given only one chance. One chance to experience life, one chance to relate to others, one chance to truly care and love. Material success, education, travel, physical health and beauty, status, power, all of these fade in the face of the power of care for another.

"You are all business persons who understand the importance of a bank account. Consider a true friendship as an account into which both friends constantly make deposits of memories, feelings, respect, and understanding. This joint memory bank contains thousands of words, smiles, meanings, incidents, places; it contains facts and figures as well as sights and sounds, smells, and touches of the relationship. Both partners constantly deposit into the common account—consciously or unconsciously the account accumulates. The memory bank grows with time, erases the bad memories, and augments the good. It can be drawn upon only by the two friends, either jointly or independently. While others may know about the account, even know its size, or be invited to benefit from it, its true value is meaningful only to the two initial depositors. Years of separate lives are erased when the common account is dipped into."

Still looking straight ahead, Ernesto noticed that Hanna had her head slightly tilted down, her eyes glancing up from below, and her face lit with a distant smile. He knew she knew that he spoke to her. He continued.

"Happy is the person who has a true friend. A friend is one who uplifts, who promotes the very best; a friend is one who melds two souls into one spirit, who lives a life of grace. Such friendship will live beyond the years that slowly steal the beauty of the body; it will cause the head to be held high, and the spirit to soar. It will give happiness an almost frightening intensity, and its very existence will be sufficient to drive you. It will give you the strength to suffer the dangers of friendship; it will empower you to take the chance of experiencing its beauty.

"If there is anything I can say to you tonight it is this: listen to the voice of your heart, be true to yourself, your instincts, they are God-placed; don't let the power of cerebral analysis be the only force in your life, and don't let a temporary man-made social code override that which is permanent and therefore ultimately beautiful. Be true to your first feelings, especially as you relate to fellow travelers on this Earth for whom you care. Be true to yourself, and life will reward you richly with happiness that knows no bounds."

The speech continued, but lasted for only twenty-five minutes. It was clear to everyone that something different was taking place tonight. While it was unrehearsed and came from the innermost and struck a chord with the business community, it had very personal meaning to only two people in the room.

After the meeting, John made an announcement that all would be reimbursed their admission fee.

8

To John's amazement, the applause slowly transformed the crowd into a moving mass, moving forward, a clear sign of success. John had been sure that the approach used tonight would not result in the expected sales of books and tapes so common to the business.

Ernesto had noticed that during the applause, Hanna, too, had risen and applauded politely. As he looked at her, he saw her lips move saying, "Thank you," he was sure. He busily shook hands, smiled, autographed books, and said the expected niceties. His eyes moved over to where Hanna was to make sure she was still there. He eased in her direction while shaking hands and autographing. John finally appeared.

"I need to leave." Ernesto said it unconvincingly.

"This crowd needs you! You can't leave now!"

"Okay, would you go get the lady?"

"Wonderful speech. Would you autograph this book, please? When did you start in business? I have this problem in my business..." Ernesto's thoughts were elsewhere.

When he looked around, John and Hanna were nearby and instinctively he took her arm and pushed toward the door. John turned to the audience and announced that, "Dr. Bauman has another engagement."

Heading down the hall and around the corner, he found a secluded lounge.

"Dr. Bauman, would you please autograph my book? I did like your speech." The persistent stranger had obviously made some effort to reach them, and Ernesto obliged.

"Thank you Dr. Bauman, Mrs. Bauman."

Mrs. Bauman? What a strange sound for the two of them to hear. Neither one said anything, but reveled in the impossible what if.

"Hanna, would you come up to my room?"

It took some effort to utter the question. Was it too risqué, too threatening, too abrupt?

"Why, what for?" she questioned reluctantly, but she knew it was the expected response.

"Hanna, I do want to spend a while alone with you; I want to relive the past. I want to pretend, for just a short while, that forty years have not passed. For a few fleeting moments I want to once again experience our youth, our carefree happiness, and our innocent expectations of life ahead. I want to give you a rose, share a glass of wine with you, talk of our happiness long, long ago in a land far, far away, hold your hand—hold you."

There was no response.

"Hanna, you can trust me. You have a family, and so do I, and nothing shall happen that will compromise our existing positions."

"I trust you, but I am not sure if I can trust myself." Her blunt response took Ernesto by surprise. He rose, reached out his hand, and after a moment's hesitation and without looking at him, she took his.

The room was quiet and would remain so as assured by the "Do Not Disturb" sign Ernesto placed on the outside of the doorknob. He walked over to the window and opened the drapes all the way, allowing the lights from the Winnipeg skyline to bathe the room. From the small refrigerator he removed a bottle of red wine. He then unfolded a white placemat, stretched it over the small table, put two glasses onto it, and filled each with wine to about half. Behind the glasses, he placed a candleholder with a single tall, white candle that he lit.

"Where did you get all this?" She had been watching in surprised awe from a short distance.

"I asked the hotel management for it," he answered, as he continued making the arrangements, and without looking at her.

He then took a crystal vase, went to the bathroom, ran some water, and appeared with a tall rose placed in the vase and placed it to the left of the candle. He removed a cassette player from a drawer, inserted a tape, and started it. Moving about as though Hanna was not present, he made the boldest move as he turned out the lights, allowing the candle and the city lights from across the window provide any needed illumination.

Preparations were now complete. He looked at her, took her hand, and led her to the happy display of sight, sound, taste, and smell. The Latin harp sounds from the player drifted across the room as they had drifted for them across the city at another time and another place. He held up a glass of wine to her. As they admired the sparkle the candlelight made, transforming it into magic fluid, they tasted of its savor as its mystical power found its way through their veins. Ernesto put his glass down and lifted the rose to Hanna for her to enjoy the aroma. Her smile and closed eyes told him she liked it.

"Remember the time when we first met, and we ran to the trolley, just barely making it?" It felt good talking about the past.

"Yes, I remember. That was fun. I beat you to the trolley." He did not answer, and she continued.

"Ernesto, do you recall when my family and I were at the airport ready to migrate to Canada? You were there with me, as we sipped sodas and took a few pictures and said our good-byes. That was so sad."

There was another long silence. They sipped more wine. Their minds traveled in the past somehow carried on wings of guitar and harp sounds in the background.

"Why? What did happen to us? Why did life take this turn for us?" Even in the faint light, Ernesto now stood close enough to make out the blueness of her eyes. He gazed into that profound blue and somehow could feel his soul melting to a place where it seemed to belong.

"Your parents would have learned to like me. I may not be well educated, but I am a likeable person." Hanna's voice carried itself with a sound of certainty.

"Talking about my parents, I did call them recently and asked my dad why he had never approved of our relationship."

"And what did they say?" She was obviously curious.

"Well, I asked them to write you a letter, but send it to me, so I could read it first, and then pass it on to you. Here it is." Ernesto was glad that she took the time to read the short note, so that he did not have to talk about it.

After reading, she folded the note, returned it to Ernesto, and from her expressions he could see that she was glad that chapter was closed.

They talked about her life and his, about their families, work, friends, dreams, hopes, and disappointments. After a long silence, she said with a certain amount of resignation, "Well, it probably would not have worked out anyway."

173

"Why do you say that?" He was curious, and glad the topic had been opened.

"You wanted a smart girl."

"That's what I want to talk to you about," he replied, and he relived aloud some of the internal turmoil of some forty years ago.

"No, I did not want a smart girl—I wanted you. I wanted your happy outlook on life, your native intelligence, your carefree spirit. I was a twenty-year old lad who was caught. I was caught emotionally because I could not imagine living without you; yet, I was not given the freedom to live near you. I needed you desperately. Life without you was incomplete and meaningless. Nothing really mattered. I felt like a half person longing to be whole. I sensed no real reason to live unless it was with you.

"But, I was so many miles from you and had no way to get to you. I was trapped in one place, could not see you, hold you, kiss you, talk with you, and make plans with you.

"I was caught financially with absolutely no money if we had decided to get married. Then I was also caught in a social turmoil lingering from the days in the country down south where the message was to get a girl with education.

"I've been thinking I should perhaps have been much more risky and bold and have gone with the leading of my heart, rather than the reasoning of the mind—come what may. You were—and always will be—my first true love. Ours was a genuine, passionate, innocent love."

"Yes, we did have an intensely happy relationship," she agreed.

They felt uncontrollably pulled toward each other and a second youth seemed to sparkle in their eyes. Their presence with each other, their talk, and their reminiscing relit in their hearts the cold ashes of a forgotten passion. He again saw in her still deep blue eyes that personal charm, that tenderness of her femininity. Though their friendship had been interrupted by decades, they had found the essence of human connectedness. But it appeared that the uncertainty of the future intensified their hearts' return to the past.

Overjoyed, yet tormented by remembrances, two sad friends succumbed to the delirium of long ago love. Without talking, both wished that the past somehow was not true, that life lay ahead, that springtime was still to come. Driven by interior fires, they sought for

174

paths to the past where youth could be recovered. They found in each other loving friends, yet were so alone as they navigated against the current of time. Two earthly creatures spent themselves in the useless effort to find the sea of forgetting.

"You know, in the past few months I have often dreamed about you, looked at the old pictures of us. I have cried and I wake up calling your name." His soul was baring itself.

Silently they waited a long time thinking about "what ifs."

"I need to tell you something." She seemed mysterious.

"Something I should have told you a long, long time ago. Perhaps early on in our relationship would have been best. But I didn't... I couldn't... I was going to tell you when I planned to visit you in the U.S., back forty years ago. I didn't come. Then it seemed that it was too late." She halted between sentences and appeared to wait for a reaction from him. He did not respond, so she continued.

"I was your first love, but you were not my first love." Again, she waited. No answer.

"I knew someone in our settlement for a brief time. He was older, was handsome, and mesmerized the girls. I didn't know he had a girlfriend, yet he came to see me, too. I knew that this could never lead to anything serious, so I just let it happen. We started kissing lightly at first, then intensely, and one thing led to another. I protested a bit, but not really. I liked the attention I was getting from this twenty-two-year-old cowboy who came riding down the street on a proud horse just to see me. I was fifteen."

"And you 'knew' each other—in the Biblical sense." He said it almost matter of factly.

"How did you know? Are you just guessing?"

"I learned it a few months ago. The cowboy you are talking about, he married his girlfriend, and they now live in the U.S. They've since divorced. His former wife is a writer, and she called me late one night and told me."

"I am so sorry. I should have told you, but I was afraid you would leave me. I did not want that. I thought I would tell you sometime. I never did. And I am sorry."

"Hanna, I have forgiven you—and so has God."

Their empty glasses now set aside; he took her into his arms and felt the warmth of her arms around him. The effect of the wine had warmed their veins as their arms now warmed their bodies. They stood there holding each other a long time, then slowly began to move in step with the haunting music from a country far away.

9

Ernesto took her home. She seemed tired but radiated an external joy and an inner peace. All during the taxi ride through town, they quietly rediscovered the beauty of close friendship, which comes when silence feeds memories.

On her front porch, they talked a bit longer.

"I am really tired," she said.

She lifted her eyes, took his face in the palms of her hands, and held it at a distance so as to study it.

She noticed how it had matured well. That somewhat awkward facial bone structure was still there, and so were the intense brown eyes speaking of an inner drive and determination. The four creases across his forehead, a trademark even in his youth, were now deeper furrows, and longer lines. Other wrinkles had found their proper places on that familiar face. She studied his hair, once a sharp brown color, now still full but mellowed in color. He had always fussed about his unruly hair. She chuckled as she remembered how he had always tried to control his cowlick using soap or even the juice of wild oranges. Now the hair, cut in the longer style, lay in place, thinner, gentler, and a distinguished gray going on white. She delighted in his well-disciplined 6-1 frame, and his middle-aged handsomeness obviously enhanced by regimented physical exercises.

Without comment, she turned his face, placed a good night kiss on his right cheek, and disappeared into the door.

"I'll see you in the morning?"

She appeared not to hear him.

Ernesto had difficulty going to sleep. He thought of the woman lying in a bed some six miles across town. How different paths destiny had taken their two lives; yet throughout all, there remained a bond of understanding. Out the window, he noticed the moon competing with the ominous looking, dark, cloud-covered sky.

It was three in the morning when the phone rang.

"Hello, is this Dr. Bauman?"

"Yes, who is it?"

"I am Angela Bender, Hanna is my mother. You know my mother, no?"

"Yes I do. What's happened?"

"We had to take her to the hospital, again. She's had a viral heart infection, rheumatic fever, for some years now, you know. It doesn't look good. She's asked for you."

"Where are you?"

As the cab raced across town, he noticed those full clouds now readying to shed their hold. The first drops of the oncoming rain wet his clothes as he entered the hospital.

In the room, he found Hanna's bed surrounded by four young people. He quietly introduced himself and shook their hands, and then they left the room.

Hanna raised herself against the end of the bed, smiled, and stretched out her long, white arms. She looked the peace of a person having arranged all matters of conscience. They embrace in a way that seemed to bridge a forty-year gap and reach forward to a lifetime.

"Ernesto, do you remember long ago when we went on a youth picnic and walked up high above the waterfalls?"

"Yes, I do."

"Do you remember the many different waterfalls, but they all fell into the same gorge below forming a single stream?"

He continued listening.

"Ernesto, we've built a citadel with a shared memory bank for just the two of us. Like the tracks of a railroad, close up our lives are a separate two, but beyond the horizon, where they stretch out of view, what was two has become one.

"But for now we are separate lives. Should we really insist on recalling what no longer exists? We can't reach back. In so trying, we might lose both the present and the future. The Hanna of the 50s and 60s represented youth, beauty, freedom from responsibility, un-attachment. That Hanna does not exist. Let us use the past to grow strong into the future. Genuine maturity has gracious poise rooted in the charms of youth.

"Well over a third of a century ago, life was unfair to both of us, but we are now better and stronger because of it and are within reach of the flowering of a mature spirit. Life is short and soon passes. In

178

heaven, we will be reunited and we'll love each other as the angels do. For now, give your love to your family."

Ernesto opened the top drawer of the nightstand and found a German Bible, still used in many of Winnipeg's hospitals. He opened to Psalm 23.

Der Herr ist mein Hirte;
mir wird nichts mangeln.
Er weidet mich auf einer grünen Aue
und führet mich zum frischen Wasser.
Er erquicket meine Seele;
er führet mich auf rechter Strasse
um seines Namens willen.
Und ob ich schon wanderte im finsteren Tal,
fürchte ich kein Unglück;
denn du bist bei mir,
dein Stecken und Stab trösten mich.
Du bereitest vor mir einen Tisch
im Angesicht meiner Feinde.
Du salbest mein Haupt mit Öl
und schenkest mir voll ein.
Gutes und Barmherzigkeit
werden mir folgen mein Leben lang,
und ich werde bleiben
im Hause des Herrn immerdar.

He then said a prayer he had learned from his mother:

Christi Blut und Gerechtigkeit,
Das ist mein Schmuck und Ehrenkleid.
Damit will ich vor Gott bestehen,
Wenn ich zum Himmel werde eingehen.

Then in an ever so gentle move, she took his hand and kissed it. It was as though the angels sang and God smiled. They were holding each other with a joy that erased time and created a feeling of belonging since the beginning of time. Their joined hands seemed to spell remembrances, remorse, forgiveness, and a new found happiness for two of God's creatures. Healing took place and a spiritual anchoring was securely established through deep roots and freeing wings.

"Please call the children."

As they came in, she embraced and kissed each one of them in turn.

"This is Ernesto I told you about, a friend of mine from a long time ago." The children nodded.

She then motioned for Ernesto to come, who had retreated to the back of the room. She embraced him, too, and he heard her faint voice saying, "I'll see you in the morning."

Then he noticed her grip loosening, but he continued to hold on. Her arms slowly slid across his back, falling limp onto the sheet. Her head leaned sideways... He held in his arms the lifeless body of what had given him life and boundless happiness. Resting the body on the pillow, he placed a kiss on her forehead and returned to the back of the room. Hanna was no more. The children came and caressed what had been their mother.

The storm outside raged in vicious fury. Ernesto went to the window, opened the drapes, and saw a courtyard filled with trees in full white bloom reaching right up to his window. Tormented by the rain, wind, and hail he watched as millions of white flowers shook in violent agony, resonating the give and take of nature's outbursts. Many branches had broken, leaving the fresh, white, wet blossoms without a source of life. He then carefully opened the window, reached out, and took a small blooming branch. Returning to that bed without life, he placed the white flowers into the folded hands of his departed.

He silently embraced each of the four crying youth and said:

"A God-sent angel came to touch my life, and she has now returned to heaven." Outside the agonized sea of white trees continued to shake in uncontrolled convulsions. All stood there, crying silently, and embracing each other. Mother was gone.

Angela introduced him to the others.

"This is Raymond, my older brother, and Roland, my younger one."

"And who is this fine young man?" Ernesto inquired.

"It is my boyfriend, Bruce."

"Ah, nice, have you known each other for a long time?"

"Two happy years."

"Tell me, did you two have your mother's blessing?"

"Oh, yes sir. She was so glad for us."

"And your parents, Bruce, do you have their blessing?"

"Oh yes, we're making plans to be married next summer."

"Tell me, are you first loves?"

Two pairs of eyes looked at each other and nodded intensely.

"Do not give up your first love. The seed that sprouts from first love is strong and everlasting. In the ravages of time the plant that is sent forth from that seed may be hurt, damaged, or even chopped, but its roots go deep and stay to sprout again. First love is God's way of giving us a glimpse of what heaven is like."

"Mom told us about the friendship you two had. Would you tell us about it some time?" Angela seemed genuinely interested.

"Ah, but of course. I'd love to do that. Let's pick a beautiful spring day out in a park full of white blossoms. Is that a deal?"

"It's a deal."

"Oh, Angela, I see from your jacket you have lettered. What sport are you in?" Ernesto could have guessed the answer.

"I'm in track and cross country, and I love it."

"And she's the fastest member of the team." Bruce's eyes boasted with glee.

10

Again, as so many times before, Ernesto sat in an airplane. But this trip was different. It was a ten-hour night trip heading south to the land of his youth. Yes, many times before had he taken this same trip. There had been the happy times when he took his family to visit the land of his birth, to get to know its people and his kin. There had been the many times when he traveled on business as consultant to agencies and institutions or as conference and workshop leader. The lands, people, and costumes were as familiar as his own home. Here he did feel at home. He liked that feeling.

But this time he flew alone—with no family, tourism, or business purpose. The cruising altitude and moonless night had blurred the landscape below into a uniform whole. He felt no urge to sleep and spent the night looking out the window—seeing nothing but feeling much.

The early morning hours were announced by the red of the impending sunrise. That deep red was matched only by the redness of the familiar earth below now closing in, in preparation for landing. He always marveled at the beautiful contrast of clear blue sky and the intense red earth of the tropics. Once again, the approach awoke in him feelings of coming home. On past trips he had always known that his father would be waiting at the terminal. He always anticipated the hearty welcome, the trip into town, the welcome from his mother, the meals she prepared, the visit with friends, the feeling of being home. But today his father would not be at the airport. No one knew of Ernesto's coming. He had come for a very private mission.

The red earth was now very close. Small farmsteads became distinct, palm trees dotted the countryside, and cars and people were rushing about. Home. His heart beat faster, sadder.

With only one handbag, he cleared costumes quickly and was on his way. He instructed the cab driver to take him to Avenida Santísimo Scaramento and to do so by starting at the intersection of Mariscal Lopez and then heading north. The driver engaged in small talk but soon noticed that Ernesto was not in a mood to talk and so the ride was quiet, as he wanted it to be. Once at the intersection, Ernesto asked the driver to please drive very slowly. Ernesto looked both ways. Much had changed, but some familiar old houses still stood, now dwarfed by modern mansions. But the road contour had not changed.

"When we get to the top of the hill where you see those trees, please stop and wait."

"Okay, señor."

For a long time, Ernesto sat in the cab looking out the left window to the low, white washed wall. He saw the buildings and gardens beyond—now different.

He walked over to the wall, sat down, and noticed many of the familiar trees and homes no longer there. But the scented air smelled as it should and allowed him to relive past events. A group of uniformed school children ran past.

He asked the cabby to take him to the closest tram station. He loved those slow, noisy, electricity-sparking contraptions from a century gone by. The jerking and shaking trip to town took almost an hour. He enjoyed that slowness, and he took in the city morning life. There among the stylishly dressed people walked an old market woman with her fruit and vegetable wares in a large, heavy basket balanced on her head. She stopped door-to-door offering her goods. The wild *apepú* orange trees still stood lining the streets. Many had knurled trunks, the scars of a city's civilization. Their golden fruits filled the trees yet were ignored by all. The familiar fruit juice stands still seemed to offer the same concoction as always. People stopped for a quick drink and went on. With the onset of the tropical winter the *chivatos* trees were filled with their blossoms. Ernesto could sense winter in the air.

He checked into a hotel and went to sleep without calling friends or relatives. His mission was otherwise.

In the early evening, he walked to do what he had come to do. From the intersection of Yegros and Antequera streets, he began to slowly walk north up the incline of Antequera Street. He stopped every twenty paces to take in the moment. He took in the happy chatter of children playing in their front yards under the proud and watchful eyes of their parents. One man waved at him as he passed.

Off in the distance somewhere he heard a harp plucking out the tune of *India,* that most famous of all local harp tunes. Yes, this was the home of his youth.

He had now come to within a block of his destination, The Angel statue. A young couple came around the corner heading for The Angel. As he arrived on the upper platform, his eyes searched for "their" spot. No one was close to it. That is where Ernesto remained for the next hour. Much had changed. Trees had grown where there were none before. Spotlights lit up the statue giving it new brilliance. High rise buildings appeared to encroach into The Angel's domain.

But most things had not changed. To his left stood that mighty column holding The Angel high up in the air. The Angel still stood perched on the toes of its left foot, spreading its wings, and as if in a blessing, held the right hand over those below. On the opposite side of the little plaza was a pair of lovers. The young man had his arm around her shoulder and seemed to whisper into her ear. Her smile indicated satisfaction. Down a little ways was another couple kissing in tender embrace.

It was a beautiful, though crisp early winter evening. He could smell the *chivatos* flowers nearby, and the haunting harp tunes oscillated through the night from somewhere far off. He let his eyes wander to the city below. How peaceful it lay there. In the far distance, one could make out the mighty river and the harbor bay with its occasional ships moving to and from anchor. It was that harbor where they had often gone on moonlit or moonless evenings, enjoying the ships and, yes, always kissing. A third couple, six or seven levels below, was enjoying the same view.

Ernesto closed his eyes for a long time reliving past memories. He thought, *Does anything around here remember the unfolding of a great love story long ago? If this monument could only speak!* Many cold winds had blown past this column since the days when it was silent witness to the flowering union in the making. The column did not speak. It remained as quiet as Hanna now lay asleep.

The cold south breeze chilled his neck and he pulled his coat tighter. From his pocket he produced a stone chisel and a hammer and began to carve deep and long into the flat base of the column. The pounding sounds echoed into the neighborhood and slowly the surface yielded the impression: H A N N A. He looked up the pedestal to watch the statue of The Angel some forty feet above. It pointed to heaven as it always had. He noticed a white turtledove perched at The Angel's feet. He watched it for a long time. Then, without warning, it spread its wings and flew up into the night sky in the direction of the Southern Cross. From the Cathedral below, the heavy sounds of the Maria Angola bell tolled in the direction The Angel was pointing.

Ernesto took off his coat, held it for a moment as though placing it on someone's shoulders, and then laid it over the stone wall in front of him. He walked a few paces behind him to break off a small branch of white flowers, then lifted one side of the coat and placed the flowers inside—right next to the pocket that held the card with the inscription: "I'll see you in the morning."

Turning south, he walked into the cold, winter wind never to return again.

At home again, he kissed his wife and held her in a long embrace. Then, hand in hand, they walked silently and for a long time in a nearby park. As they returned, Ernesto leaned over to her and whispered, "Thank you!"

Riwen Forester

About the Author

Riwen Forester is a professor and academic administrator at a major Midwestern university. He has published much in his scientific field; however, this is his first novel.

He lives happily with his wife of over 40 years.

You may contact the author at: 1st Books Library, 2595 Vernal Pike, Bloomington, IN 47404. 866-577-8877. E-mail: 1stbooks@1stbooks.com.

Printed in the United States
16593LVS00003B/259